Their Favorite Game

A BROTHER'S BEST FRIENDS ROMANCE

CALLIE SKY

Their Favorite Game

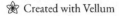

To my husband for loving me and helping me write about women being banged by multiple men.

Trigger Warnings –
These may contain spoilers

If any of these are a trigger please do not read this book. There are so many other amazing books out there. No book is worth it.

Although this is a lighter book, there are still triggers.

Sex scenes, sex scenes with multiple partners, back door play. Loss of mother due to cancer.

These next few are quickly mention, but still there. Loss of brother due to suicide, substance abuse.

CHAPTER 1

Mal

MY VISION BLURRED. THE BEERS WERE GOING DOWN too smoothly. The people dancing were no more than fuzzy silhouettes. Pushing down the turning in my stomach, I joined my friend on the dance floor.

Sammy Lane, my bestie of eighteen years. We had met in the hospital nursery, our mom's shared a room, and we had grown up side-by-side ever since. When the music started to play, Sammy grabbed me and spun us around in an awkward circle, her body pressed tight against mine. Although we were notorious for our lack of dancing finesse, we were determined to enjoy the moment.

In high school, boys never asked me to a dance. If it weren't for Sammy, I would have had zero skills when it came to having rhythm. It wasn't like I had any coordination. There was a particular homecoming that I thought one of my brother's best friends would ask me to. They didn't.

"You alright, Mal?" Sammy's voice was slurred. She swayed back and forth, causing her crop top to rise, and her breasts threatened to fall out.

"They are here!" I shouted over the drum of the music.

Of course, they would show up. Why wouldn't they? It was my brother's party, and they were his best friends. All four of them had been inseparable since we were kids. As the little sister, I was ignored, but that didn't stop me from fantasizing about them.

"Girl, go talk to them." Sammy swayed her body.

"No, no. I'm good." I matched her beat. My body fell into the rhythm even though my mind thought of them.

A girl in nothing but a bikini and flip-flops walked by carrying a tray of shooters. "Shots, girls?"

"Absolutely." Sammy grabbed two pink tubes and flicked her curly blonde hair out of the way. I shot it down with her and concentrated on the music as I lost myself in it momentarily. The alcohol made me more daring than usual, but the idea of going over to my brother's friends was nerve-wracking. They were all older than me by two years, and I didn't want to come across as the little sister trying to hang out with them.

Sammy didn't seem to care, though. She pulled me towards them, and I stumbled a little, my head still fuzzy. My brother's friend, Jake, caught me before I fell and held me steady.

"Easy there, little sis," he said with a grin. Jake was the closest to my age in the group, but he still seemed much more relaxed than me. "You've had a little too much to drink, huh?"

"I'm fine," I said, but my voice was slurred, and I knew I didn't sound convincing.

"Let's get you some water," he suggested, and I let him lead me to the side of the room where a cooler was set up with drinks. He handed me a bottle of water, and I took a few sips, hoping I didn't look like a camel gulping water.

"Thanks," I said, looking up at him. Jake was tall and lean, with shaggy brown hair and bright blue eyes that always seemed to twinkle with mischief. He wore a tight black t-shirt that showed off his defined biceps and tattoos peeking out from under the sleeves.

"No problem." Jake smiled at me with a crooked grin, making my heartbeat hasten. "You having fun at the party?"

"I guess," I said, slightly shy under his gaze. "It's not my scene, but Sammy wanted to come."

Jake nodded, his eyes scanning the room. "Yeah, it's a little wild for me, too. But it's all in good fun."

We stood there for a moment, taking in the scene. My brother, Frankie, set up these parties once a month. He would rent a warehouse or somewhere else obscure and charge people an entrance fee. Even at twenty, he was an entrepreneur. I never attended his parties. Too many people always made me anxious. Tonight, I was only here because Sammy begged me. I wouldn't have needed so much convincing if I had known I would have been in a corner alone with Jake.

Jake's eyes met mine, and we locked gazes. There was a moment of silence between us before he leaned in closer to me. "You know, I always thought you were too good for this scene."

My chest tightened as my heart began to flutter. Was he flirting with me?

"You're smart, beautiful, and talented," he continued. "You should be out there conquering the world, not partying with us losers."

A wave of disappointment washed over me. Was this his way of telling me he wasn't interested? I had always thought he was perfect and dreamed of him noticing me, not just as Frankie's little sister. But now that he was, it only made me question if he was into me.

"Thanks, Jake," I said, trying to keep the disappointment out of my voice. "That's really nice of you to say."

He sensed my disappointment because he placed a hand

on my arm. "Hey, don't take it the wrong way. I didn't mean anything by it. You're Frankie's sister and practically family."

I turned to rejoin Sammy on the dance floor. Rex and Matty were laughing it up with her. I tried to look unfazed. I had no right to be jealous. Seriously, what kind of person crushed on all three of their brother's best friends? Ugh, what was wrong with me?

"Hey Mal, I grabbed you another shot," Sammy said when I joined her. I took it without hesitation.

The shot burned down my throat, and I relished the feeling of the alcohol hitting my system. But even as I took the shot, I couldn't stop the pang of jealousy as I watched Sammy with Rex and Matty. They were laughing and joking around like they didn't have a care in the world. Why couldn't I be a part of that? I had known them just as long as Sammy, but they all called me 'little sis.' It was worse than being friend-zoned.

"Hey, let's dance," Sammy grabbed my hand and pulled me deeper into the dance floor, away from the men.

I let her drag me along, my mind still preoccupied with thoughts of Jake and Frankie's other friends. They were all so cool and confident, while I was a nervous wreck half the time.

As we danced, I caught a glimpse of Jake across the room. He was laughing and joking around with his friends, his eyes scanning the crowd. For a moment, our gazes locked again, and goosebumps ran up my arms.

"Why don't you tell them how you feel?" Sammy shouted over the music.

"Not gonna happen!" I shouted back.

My head spun. The music pounded against my chest. Everything in the room was spinning. Shit, maybe I had drunk too much. As I stumbled towards the exit to get some fresh air, Jake appeared before me. His muscular arms caught me before I hit the ground.

"Whoa there." He steadied me with his hands. "Are you okay?"

I looked up at him. His face zoomed in and out. "I think I had too much to drink," I slurred.

"Let me take you outside." He guided me to the door. "You need some fresh air."

Once outside, I took deep breaths, gasping for air. I couldn't stop the spinning, but the nausea calmed down. Jake stood beside me, his hand on my back.

"Feeling better?" he asked.

I nodded, grateful for his help. "Thanks, Jake. You're always so kind to me."

He smiled at me, his eyes twinkling in the moonlight. "Of course, Mal. I care about you. You know that, right?"

Yeah, as a little sister. I kept my mouth shut instead of saying what I wanted to. It also helped to keep the bile down that started threatening to creep up, despite my desperately trying to keep it down.

I swayed and went to sit down. Rex's arms wrapped around me. "Hey, little sis, it's okay. I got you." His blonde hair glowed against the moonlight.

Squinting against the darkness, I realized Matty was with them as well. I was outside alone with all three of them. Clamping my mouth shut, I tried not to say anything.

But as the alcohol clouded my judgment, the words slipped out before I could stop them. "You know, sometimes I wish you guys didn't just see me as Frankie's little sister," my voice was barely above a whisper.

They exchanged a look, and Rex spoke up. "Of course, we don't just see you as that, Mal. You're our friend too."

Matty nodded in agreement, his hand resting on my shoulder. "Yeah, we care about you, kid."

Kid? Kid? See, that was the problem, and they didn't see it. I was always the kid, the little sister. Nothing more to them. I opened my mouth to yell, and bile slammed into my throat. No, not in front of them, please.

Rex must have sensed my unease because he pulled away slightly and looked at me with concern. "You okay, Mal? You look like you're about to be sick."

I shook my head, trying to fight off the nausea that was building in my stomach. "I'm fine," I said weakly.

Matty stepped forward and placed a hand on my shoulder. "Do you need us to take you home?" he asked.

I shook my head again, but the nausea was too intense. I doubled over and vomited on the grass, my body heaving with effort.

"Shit," Jake whispered. "We need to get you home." At least, I thought it was him. Words swam in and out of view, shivers ran up my spine, and the air was so heavy I couldn't breathe.

Arms wrapped around me and lifted me. I was vaguely aware of Rex and Matty on either side of me, guiding me toward their car. I was too dizzy to resist, too sick to protest.

As we drove through the dark streets, I leaned my head against the window. I made a fool of myself in front of them. Now not only was I the little sister, but I was also the idiot who couldn't handle her alcohol.

But despite my embarrassment, I was grateful for their help. They didn't have to take care of me, but they did. They could have easily told my brother and made him deal with me.

As we pulled up to my house, I stumbled out of the car, my head spinning. Rex and Matty helped me up the steps to my front door, and I fumbled with my keys until Jake took them from me and opened the door.

"Thanks," I said, my voice barely above a whisper.

Jake smiled at me, his eyes warm and kind. "No problem, Mal. Just take care of yourself, okay?"

I nodded. "You guys are the best."

Rex and Matty grinned at me, their faces illuminated by the porch light. "We know," Rex said, ruffling my hair affectionately. "Now go get some rest. We'll see you soon."

Words fumbled out of my mouth, most of them incoherent. All of them were things I shouldn't have said. I wasn't even positive I had spoken out loud. "Hot, all of you, stay, be here." I tried inviting them in but couldn't fully get a sentence out.

"We should get her inside." Matty turned to his friends.

Jake whispered something that sounded vaguely like 'rules.' Words spun around my head, and sounds zoomed away from me. I was pretty sure I was already dreaming or on the verge of blacking out.

Rex nodded to me and walked back to the car. The other two followed him, and I watched them like a fool. For once, I had liquid courage and was too drunk to say what I had been trying to tell them for years.

I stumbled inside, both embarrassed and grateful. As I made my way to my bedroom, I couldn't help but be disappointed. They were always kind to me, but as Rex had said: they saw me as their little sister. It was hopeless to want anything more.

But as I collapsed onto my bed, I couldn't stop thinking about them. As much as I tried to convince myself it was just a childish crush, I knew it was more. They were all I ever thought about. I never had a boyfriend because no one had ever grabbed my attention the way they did. If I could get over them, I could find someone and stop being the only eighteen-year-old virgin in Western New York.

With those thoughts swirling around in my head, I drifted into a fitful sleep, my dreams filled with images of the three men and me tangled up in each other's arms. It was a fantasy I knew could never be a reality, but it made for one hell of a dream.

CHAPTER 2

Mal

THE FOLLOWING DAY, I WOKE UP WITH A POUNDING headache and overwhelming regret. My embarrassing behavior from last night was fresh in my mind, and I cringed at the thought of facing Jake, Rex, and Matty again. Maybe I could manage to avoid them forever.

As I stumbled downstairs to the kitchen, I found my brother already there, sipping coffee and reading the newspaper. He had the same green eyes as me, but his hair was pitch black and was never out of place. Frankie took care of himself and always had the girls chasing after him.

"Morning, Mal." Frankie looked up from his paper.

"Morning," I grumbled, grabbing a glass of water and a Tylenol.

Frankie raised an eyebrow at me. "Rough night?"

I groaned, my head throbbing. "You could say that."

Frankie chuckled, his eyes crinkling with amusement at my disheveled appearance. "Well, at least you had fun, right?"

I scowled at him, not in the mood for his teasing. "It wasn't that fun."

Frankie shrugged. "If you say so. Did you see Jake, Rex, and Matty last night?"

"Um, I mean, yeah. They were at the party. I had to leave," I said, plopping beside him.

"They left without saying anything to me. I saw Rex and Matty talking to Sammy. Maybe one of them left with her." He shook his head. "It's not my business, and I know she is your best friend, but she chews up guys and spits them out."

Shit, Sammy. I grabbed my phone and went to text her.

There was already a message from her.

SAMMY

> I really hope you banged them

> > Did not. See you at work

> I'm disappointed. I hooked up with some rando last night. I'll tell you all about it later.

I grabbed my face and squeezed. Of course, she did. I was still a virgin, but she was always having sex. If I had a touch of her confidence, I wouldn't be such an awkward weirdo. There was also the slight problem that I was infatuated with three men who were off-limits.

Trying to push those thoughts aside, I focused on making breakfast for myself and Frankie. As I cracked eggs into a bowl, my mind drifted back to the previous night. Despite my embarrassment and regret, I couldn't get Jake, Rex, and Matty off my mind.

But that was a dangerous path to go down. They were my brother's friends, and I didn't want to risk ruining their friendship over some stupid crush. Plus, I didn't even know if they were interested in me that way. Who was I kidding? They weren't into me. They made that clear.

Frankie got up from the table and grabbed his bag as I finished cooking breakfast. "I'm heading to work. You gonna be okay?"

I nodded. "Yeah, I'll be fine."

But as soon as Frankie left, I wanted to crawl back into bed and stay there forever. I had a few hours before work and nothing to do but replay the events of last night. I was such a fool.

I spent the rest of the morning trying to distract myself with mindless activities, but my thoughts kept drifting back to the three men. I wondered if they ever thought about me romantically or if I was just their little sister figure.

Before I knew it, it was time to head to work. I worked at a small diner in town and enjoyed the simplicity of serving tables and chatting with customers. It was only temporary until I could pay for cosmetology school. I couldn't concentrate on anything today. My thoughts were too distracting.

As I worked, I noticed a group of guys come in. One was tall with shaggy brown hair, one was blonde with a smile that could melt any heart, and the last one had dark hair that hung in his mischievous eyes. My heart raced as I recognized Jake, Rex, and Matty. They smiled when they saw me, and my face flushed with embarrassment.

"Hey, Mal," Jake said, leaning against the counter. "Table for three."

"Can you join us? We are celebrating." Matty slapped Rex on the back.

"Gotta work, but what are you guys celebrating?" I asked as I grabbed three menus and walked them over to a booth in my section.

"Our boy here got into Florida. He got a full-ride scholarship." Jake smiled as he sat down.

Rex had been playing football since before he could walk. An injury in high school had him on the bench during the season when scouts picked up their new players. He had to go to community college and work hard at getting a scout to notice him. It's impossible to be picked up in your sophomore year, but he did it.

"That's amazing, congrats!" I said, genuinely happy for him.

The guys ordered their food and drinks, and I tried to act normal as I served them. But every time Jake touched my arm, Rex grinned at me, or Matty made a joke, my heart raced with excitement.

As the night wore on, the restaurant cleared out, and I found myself sitting with the guys at their booth, sipping coffee. We discussed Rex's college plans, and I shared my aspirations of becoming a cosmetologist.

"That's so cool, Mal," Jake said, his hand resting on my thigh. "You'll be great at it."

A shiver ran down my spine at his touch, and I couldn't help but wonder if it meant something more. But then again, maybe he was just being friendly.

"It sucks that this is our last summer together." Matty tore at the wrapper from his straw.

"Huh?" I chewed my lip. Everyone grows up and moves on; I knew that. I just hadn't thought of all three of them leaving.

"Yeah, Rex got the scholarship. I leave for New York in September to help run my dad's company." Jake smiled, but it fell flat. "And our little genius here, Matty, will teach Geometry at Harvard."

Matty graduated high school at fourteen and college two years after. He had a photographic memory and was a genius in mathematics, hence his early graduation and the invitation to teach at Harvard. I stared at my empty cup, hoping they didn't see the tears that threatened to leak out.

"I'm going to miss you guys," I said, my voice cracking with each word.

Jake's hand squeezed my thigh. "We'll miss you too, Mal. But we'll always be friends, no matter where we end up."

I nodded. Part of me was happy that we would always be friends, but another part wished for something more.

As the night wore on, the guys paid their tab and got up to leave. Jake leaned in and kissed me on the cheek, sending a jolt of electricity through me.

"Goodnight, Mal," he said, his hand lingering on my shoulder. "If you are bored later we will be at Outskirts bar tonight. We can get you in."

"Goodnight," I replied, watching them leave with a heavy heart.

As I cleaned up the restaurant and got ready to go home, I couldn't shake the thought of this being our last summer together and my last chance to express my feelings for them.

"What's wrong?" Sammy asked as she filled the ketchup bottles.

"They are all leaving," I sighed and turned away from her. "All three of them are going off to become successful, and I'm gonna be in this crappy little town cutting hair until I die of cancer like my mom."

Sammy put her hand on my shoulder. "Hey, don't talk like that. You have so much potential. And who knows, maybe something will happen between you and one of them before they leave, or all of them."

I shook my head, defeated. "I doubt it. They see me as Frankie's little sister. Plus, they can have any girl they want. Why would they want me?"

Sammy rolled her eyes. "Oh please, Mal. You're beautiful and smart and funny. They would be lucky to have you."

I smiled weakly but didn't say anything. As much as I

appreciated her words, I couldn't help but feel like she was just being nice.

"So, what happened last night?" I asked, changing the subject.

"Well." A mysterious smile spread across her face. "You remember Travis Montgomery from lit class?"

"You didn't?" I gasped.

"Oh, I did. I did a lot." Sammy twisted her body back and forth. "He bent me over his bed and..."

"Okay, I don't need the details," I interrupted, heat rising to my cheeks.

Sammy just laughed. "Sorry, Mal. I just wanted to cheer you up. Maybe you should find a guy to help take your mind off things."

I frowned. "I don't think that's the solution."

"Suit yourself," she said, shrugging. "I just think the best way to get over a guy is to get under another one. Trust me on that. I crushed on a guy so bad and thought we were gonna start a relationship, then bam, nothing. So I banged a few guys and felt better."

"You were gonna start a relationship? With who?" I placed my hand on my hip. She was my best friend. If she was serious about a guy, I would know.

"Ladies, hurry up. I don't wanna stay all night!" Barb, the manager, shouted from the back of the restaurant.

As I walked home that night, I couldn't stop thinking about the guys and the possibility of something happening between us. Maybe Sammy was right. Perhaps I needed to take a chance and make a move. It was risky, but what did I have to lose?

When I got home, I found a note from Frankie saying he wouldn't be home until morning. Perfect, I thought, feeling a rush of excitement. I quickly changed into something more comfortable and headed out to find the guys.

They had invited me here but I still felt slightly stalkerish showing up. My heart raced as I made my way over to them, unsure of what to say.

"Hey guys," I said, trying to sound casual.

"Mal!" Jake grinned, grabbing a chair and pulling it up to the table. "Come sit with us."

I sat and adjusted my position multiple times before I forced myself to stop. "So, what are you guys up to?"

"Drinking and celebrating Rex's scholarship," Matty said, slurring his words.

"I can see that," I laughed. "I don't know how you guys can drink after last night. My head is still pounding."

Jake leaned in close to me, brushing his hand against my arm. "I can help make that headache go away," he whispered.

My heart skipped a beat as I met his gaze, and a jolt of electricity passed between us. Was he flirting with me? Or was it just the alcohol talking?

"How's that?" I asked, trying to keep my voice steady.

"Sex always worked for me," Matty grinned.

"Sex works for everything." Jake winked at me.

My heart slammed into my chest. This was why I was here, right? I knew a real relationship wasn't a possibility with them. With them all leaving, we only had the summer. Could this be real, or were they drunk?

"Unless it's before a big game. Then your head gets foggy, and you don't play as well." Rex chugged his beer and slammed it down.

I laughed, thankful for the change of subject. "Well, I guess that's good to know."

We continued talking and drinking, the guys sharing stories of their high school days and what they hoped to accomplish. As the night wore on, I became more attracted to Jake. His touch, his smile, and how he looked at me made my heart race excitedly. Honestly, I wanted all three of them, but Jake kept giving me attention.

"Hey, Mal," Jake said, leaning close to me. "Can I talk to you outside for a second?"

"Sure." My stomach flipped as if a butterfly sanctuary moved in.

CHAPTER 3

Jake

When I was nine, my mother moved me from New York City to Maryvale, New York. A small town in upstate New York. At least to me, it was small. To everyone who lived here, it was larger than most neighboring towns.

I hated my mother for leaving my father. To me, he had everything. He owned a marketing business that he started from the ground up. It was a million-dollar company that afforded us a life I enjoyed at nine. It wasn't enough for my mom.

Being rich and living in New York City was fabulous. I had a personal driver that would take me to school. Of course, my school was Marin Academy, home to children of politicians and celebrities. The birthday parties that I went to rivaled ordinary people's weddings. I never wanted for anything, and yeah, I guess I was spoiled. Nothing could have fixed the hole in my chest from leaving Manhattan. At least, that was what I thought until I met my best friend.

We moved right next to the Andersons. They had two kids, Frankie and Mallory. Frankie was nine as well, and Mallory was only seven. For the longest time, she was the annoying little sister. She always had these lopsided pigtails that would flap as she chased us up and down the street. Even when we tried to escape her, our parents would force us to watch her. I would try to tell her jokes and make her laugh as a bribe to get her to go away. One day Frankie saved up all of his lawn-mowing business money and paid a teenager to keep Mal out of our hair. I couldn't have been happier to not be bothered by her. That changed the summer she turned fifteen.

It was a hot summer day, the kind that made you want to strip down to your skivvies and lay in front of the fan all day. I was in my room when I heard a knock at my window. I looked up to see Mallory standing outside. She wore a tank top that showed off her perky breasts and shorts that barely covered her ass. At fifteen, she had grown up to be quite the stunner.

"Jake, can I come in?" she asked, her voice sweet as honey.

I hesitated for a moment, not quite sure what she was after. Mallory had always been a pest, following me and begging me to play with her. Even with her babysitters and best friend Sammy, she would find ways to try to tag along with her brother and, subsequently, me. But now, looking at her, I could see that she wasn't a little girl anymore.

"Yeah, sure," I said, opening the window and letting her climb into my room.

She sat on my bed and flipped her wavy caramel-brown hair over her shoulder. "It's so hot."

"It is." I shoved my hands into my pockets. "So, what's up?"

"Sammy is at camp. Frankie has a new girl, and I'm bored." Mal rolled over to stare at me. "Wanna hang out?"

I wanted nothing more than to hang out with her. I would have if it wasn't for the pact I made with Matty and Rex. It was a simple pact. None of us could have her. She was Frankie's little sister, and we couldn't do that to our best friend.

Mal arched her back as if tempting me to climb on top of her. There was no way she could know how fast my heart beat in my chest or how badly she was teasing me. Even though I had managed to bury myself in plenty of girls in high school, she had never even gone on a date.

"So?" Mal pushed up on her elbows and raised her eyebrows.

"Um, I can't." I grabbed the back of my neck and looked down at the floor.

"Right, no big." Mal scrambled off the bed and practically dove toward the window.

I tried to open my mouth to stop her. Hanging out with her for the day alone would have been fantastic. It also would have been dangerous. Her foot got caught up in a pile of my clothes. She leaned forward and tried to catch herself. I jumped to grab her. Glass shattered. I was too late.

Mal's arm went through my bedroom window. There was so much blood. Everything after that happened in a blur. Getting her to the hospital was the easy part. Explaining to everyone why she was in my bedroom was difficult. Everyone accused me of fooling around with her. I did have a reputation, but I would never treat Mal like she was just a fun time.

I should have hung out with her, and she wouldn't have gotten hurt.

"Hey, you wanted to talk?" Mal kicked at the gravel in the parking lot.

Her words brought me back to the present. I shook my head from side to side as if to clear it out. "Huh?"

"You said you wanted to talk. So, talk."

"I do." I stared into Mal's eyes. She had the most beautiful green eyes I have ever seen. They were a deep emerald green.

When we were together, I would lose myself in her eyes. She was intoxicating. I felt like I was high just being around her.

"Well, go ahead." She chewed her lip and averted her eyes.

"Can I take you out?" I asked. " I mean, like an actual date."

"Really? Why?" Mal kicked at more gravel.

"Remember that day you fell through my window?" I grabbed her right arm and ran my fingers along the three scars.

"Yeah, thirty-five stitches. How could I forget?" She pulled her arm away and covered the scars.

"I should have hung out with you that day. You're Frankie's sister, and man, just having you in my bedroom caused problems with him."

"So you wanna hang out now?" Mal bit her lip, and it took everything in me to not kiss her.

"Yeah."

"Okay."

"Cool. Let's go back in. Rex and Matty probably thought we left." I tossed my arm around her and led her back into the bar.

When we returned, Rex and Matty were still at the bar. They had drinks in hand and looked up when they heard us. "Where have you two been?" Rex asked.

"Just out for a walk," I said, pulling out a chair for Mallory to sit on.

We took a seat, and I ordered Mal a soda. She had no intention of drinking again anytime soon. We talked about school and our plans for the summer as we sipped our drinks.

I was so distracted by Mal that I barely talked. I could only stare at her, smile, and nod to everything she said. When she laughed and tossed her head back, the urge to grab her and pull her into the bathroom to make out was overwhelming. I wanted to see her firm breasts and touch her smooth skin.

After hours of drinks and laughter, Mal looked at me and said, "Frankie is going to kill me if I don't get home on time."

"Yeah, I should head back as well." I took a long drink of my beer.

We all stood and said our goodbyes. "I'll see you guys tomorrow," Mal waved awkwardly as she headed toward the door.

"See ya," I said, the disappointment in my voice evident.

I watched her walk away and noticed how her hips swayed back and forth as she moved. I wanted to grab them, pull her back to me, and squeeze. I had to remind myself that she wasn't mine. But I wanted her. I wanted her more than anything in the world.

CHAPTER 4

Mal

My bed was piled high with at least twenty dresses and multiple shirt and pant combinations. *What was I supposed to wear? Jake told me to dress casual, but not too casual. What did that even mean? Were jeans and a T-shirt too sloppy? Would a dress be too formal? Ugh.*

I needed help. I grabbed the phone and called Sammy. She lived a few blocks away and rushed over. The girl was always great for a fashion emergency.

Sammy walked into the house without knocking. It was a sign of true friendship. Even when my dad was home, she just walked in. My dad usually wasn't home. This time, he was out of town on a business trip, and my brother was at work, so we would be left alone to debate what to wear.

"So, what's going on?" She sat down on my bed with an air of confidence.

"Jake asked me out." I held up a dress, eyeing myself in the mirror.

"What? Finally! Tell me everything. Did you blow him yet? Will his other two hunky friends be joining you?" Sammy flopped back onto the bed, her heels digging into the mattress.

"Do you think Jake will bang you from behind while Rex and Matty watch? That would be so hot!"

"Stop it." Heat rose to my cheeks. I tossed a pink sundress at Sammy.

"I'm just saying." Sammy flung the dress to the floor. "I would do anything to have three men doting on me."

"Who wouldn't?" I laughed. "Anyway, can you help me? I don't know what to wear."

"If I was going on a date with Jake Matthews, I would wear nothing," Sammy laughed.

"I'm serious, Sammy." I raised my voice, annoyed at her flippant attitude.

"Okay, okay. What's wrong with the outfit you have on now?" She looked me up and down.

"I look like I'm going to prom." The dress was a sparkly blue number I thought was cool when I was fifteen.

"I thought hairdressers had more style." She got up and started pulling the rest of my clothes from my closet.

"Ha, you and I both know I have no style." I tossed a pair of black slacks at her.

"I wouldn't say no style." Sammy examined a retro t-shirt I got from the thrift store. "Just the style of a nineties grunge thing. Don't worry. We will get you looking sexy."

Sammy made two piles. One she claimed was an absolute no, and the other was for me to try on. The try-on pile was obscenely big and would take hours to put on.

After rummaging through the snacks and drinks in the mini-fridge that my brother had gifted me for Christmas, Sammy perched on my bed, awaiting my performance. I rolled my eyes. I should have realized this would take way longer than expected. Had I not crushed on Jake for years, I wouldn't have taken this so seriously. It was also my first date. I had been asked out by a handful of guys, but no one compared to Jake, Matty, and Rex. If it wasn't them, I didn't want it.

Outfit after outfit I tried on. Even Sammy agreed none of them had the 'look.' It wasn't like I could go out and buy a new outfit. I was saving every penny for cosmetology school. With all the medical bills my mom left behind, I couldn't borrow money from my dad.

"I give up," I said, throwing the last dress in my closet to the ground. I flopped back onto the bed and threw my arm over my eyes. "I knew this was a bad idea. I look like a preteen."

"No, you don't." Sammy patted my back. "You look beautiful."

She could say that as a friend, but I knew better. I was scared to look at myself in the mirror. My hair was in a million different directions, my makeup was smeared, and my outfit was from my freshman year of high school. I wasn't cute, I wasn't sexy, I was a mess. I was a dork.

"Mal, you're beautiful, and Jake is lucky to get a chance to go out with you." She was trying to make me feel better, but she was failing.

Sammy grabbed my arms and set me on the bed. She rummaged through the clothes one last time. Determination spread across her face. I tried to tell her it was useless, but she ignored me.

Sammy pulled a black skirt off the bed and tossed it to me. "Try this on," she said, already starting to disrobe. She took off her black lacy shirt and, standing in just her bra, held it out for me to take. Her petite frame meant the top was two sizes too small for me – my bust pushing against the fabric's limits. My cheeks flush as I realized how much cleavage I was about to expose.

So much of me wanted to hate the outfit. It was tight and revealing. I turned in the mirror multiple times, looking for an excuse to not wear it. I couldn't find any. It was perfect. I looked my age instead of like a kid playing dress up. *Hey, at least I would look hot for my date.*

"Perfect, now let's fix that hair and makeup." Sammy tossed on my retro tee and then pulled out her makeup bag from her purse. "You do realize when you get your cosmetology license, I get free haircuts for life."

I laughed as Sammy started to apply makeup to my face. I closed my eyes and let her work her magic. She was always so good at this kind of thing. In under ten minutes, she had transformed me from a dorky-looking girl to a bombshell. My cheeks were rosy, my eyes were smoky, and my lips were plump and glossy. I couldn't believe it was me in the mirror.

Sammy then reached for my hair, pulling my hair into an updo that was both elegant and sexy. It was perfect for the night ahead.

I thanked Sammy for her help and watched her leave with a smile. I was ready for my date with Jake. I was wearing something that made me feel confident and sexy. A friend like her came around once in a lifetime, and I was grateful.

As I walked out of the house, I saw Jake standing by his blue truck. He was leaning against the door, looking as handsome as ever in a leather jacket and jeans.

"Hey." I walked over to him, rubbing my sweaty palms against my skirt. Maybe there was still time to turn around and run.

"Wow, you look amazing," he said, his eyes raking over my body.

"Um..thanks," I stuttered, trying to suck in air.

Jake opened the truck door for me and helped me step up into it. I was grateful for the low heels instead of the stilettos Sammy had insisted I wear. Jake got into the driver's seat and started the engine. The truck roared to life, and he pulled out of the driveway. We drove in silence for a while. I kept clearing my throat to speak, but my mouth was so dry I couldn't get words out. He must have thought I was a walrus.

"So, where are we going?" I croaked out.

"It's a surprise," Jake smirked, keeping his eyes on the road.

I rolled my eyes. "You know I hate surprises." I bit my lip. I shouldn't have said that. It made me sound like I didn't want to go. Ugh, this dating thing was hard, and I was failing.

"Well, you'll just have to trust me." He glanced over at me, a mischievous twinkle in his eyes.

I couldn't help but smile. Jake had always been good at making me feel comfortable. Even as a kid, he was the only one to make me laugh when I was upset.

We drove for what seemed like hours, the sun setting in the sky. I had no idea where we were going, but I was excited to find out.

Finally, we pulled into a parking lot in front of a small restaurant. From the outside, I could tell this place was expensive. Like weird things on the menu, and stuff I couldn't afford. My mom had always told me to bring money on a date, never expect the man to pay. If he does great, but never depend on a man for anything.

Jake got out of the truck and quickly walked around to open my door. I stepped out and smoothed my skirt, the sweat building in my palms again. I kept my eyes on the pavement, hoping I wouldn't stumble and fall.

"Ready?" Jake asked, holding out his hand for me to take.

I nodded, taking his hand and letting him lead me into the restaurant. The hostess greeted us and showed us to our table in a cozy corner of the dimly lit dining room. The table was set with white tablecloths, candles, and a small vase of roses. Definitely way too expensive of a place for me to go.

Jake pulled out my chair, and I sat down, avoiding his gaze. I had never been to a restaurant like this before. The waiter came over to take our drink orders, and we both ordered Coke. There had been too much drinking lately.

"So, what's good here?" I asked, trying to sound casual.

Jake leaned back in his chair, a playful grin on his face.

"Everything."

"Oh." I opened the menu. I couldn't pronounce most of it and couldn't afford any of it.

"What's wrong?" He pulled the menu down from my face.

"Nothing." I averted my eyes and shuffled my feet.

"You can tell me," Jake said softly, reaching across the table to take my hand. "Is it the menu? Don't worry about it. We'll find something you like."

I sighed, slumping forward. "It's just that...I can't afford anything on here."

Jake's face softened. "This is a date. I'm paying. Get whatever you want."

"No, did you see these prices? You shouldn't be paying for this either." I pointed at a steak that was seventy-eight dollars.

"I know, and this place is the best restaurant within a hundred miles. And you deserve the best." He brought my hand to his lips and kissed my knuckles.

Sammy didn't need to put any blush on me. I was redder than a fire hydrant. My head spun as I pulled my hand back into me. The tingling of his lips against my skin lingered.

"Um, no, I can't let you do that." I scanned the menu for the cheapest item. It was a Caesar salad for fifteen dollars.

"You love my mom's pasta and meatballs, right?" Jake asked.

I nodded.

"Okay, well, she got the recipe from here. We come here for her birthday every year. She says it tastes like New York City food." He shrugged. "Anyway, she became friends with the owner, and she gave my mom the recipe."

"Really?" I squeaked. Mrs. Matthews made the best meatballs.

"Yes, so will you please let me buy you dinner?" He widened his eyes as if he was a deer in headlights.

I burst out laughing. Quickly realizing I was in a restaurant full of people, I shut my mouth. Afraid that if I opened my mouth again, that hyena noise would resurface, I nodded.

"Perfect." He waved the waitress over and ordered our food.

As we waited, a robust woman burst through the kitchen doors and made a beeline for our table. It took everything in me not to dive under the table and hide from her. She reached us and wrapped her sweaty arms around me, pulling me from my seat. I didn't know who she was or why she hugged me, but her scent of garlic and pesto was comforting.

After what must have been five awkward minutes, she plopped me back into my seat.

"Hi, I'm Gloria, and who are you?" She stuck out a chubby hand to me.

"Um, um," I rubbed the back of my neck.

"Gloria, this is Mal." Jake pointed to me. "Mal, this is the owner, Gloria."

"Hi." I grabbed her hand and shook it.

"Aren't you just beautiful?" Gloria pulled up a chair from a nearby table and sat down. "Tell me everything."

"Huh?" I stared at her.

"Like how you two met. How long you guys have been dating." Gloria clasped her hands together. "Are you going with him to New York City? Oh, is this an engagement dinner? Oh no, did I ruin it?"

"Gloria!" Jake snapped.

"Hush, I'm asking her." Gloria waved her hand at him.

"It's our first date," I whispered.

"No way." Gloria's eyes widened. "How can that be? He has never taken a girl here."

"She is special." Jake glared at Gloria. "Please, you can interrogate her when she is more prepared next time."

"Okay, I will." Gloria stood to leave. "Order the tiramisu for dessert. Dinner is on me tonight."

"Thank you," I stuttered as she left.

Jake was right about the pasta. It tasted exactly like his mom's. I barely spoke as I shoved the food in my mouth. Had I been on a date with someone else, I would have been embarrassed about my eating habits. Growing up next to Jake, I had eaten in front of him hundreds of times.

When dessert came, I had no room left for it. The waitress had sparklers in the tiramisu, which made everyone turn to us as if we were celebrating an anniversary or something special. Since everyone was looking at us, I took a bite. Then another bite. Before I knew it, I had eaten the entire delectable dessert. It was moist and sweet and tickled the senses with a hint of coffee. I loved it.

A warmth spread through my chest as I stared at Jake. I didn't have any dating experience to compare it to, but this had to be a one-of-a-kind experience. Everything with him was so easy, yet I couldn't stop thinking about Matty and Rex. Why did I have to crush on three people?

Jake took my hand as we left the restaurant and led me to his truck. He opened the door for me and helped me up before walking around to the driver's seat.

"Thank you," I said softly as he started the engine.

Jake turned to me with a smile. "For what?"

"For everything. The dinner, the surprise, Gloria, being here with me tonight. It means a lot."

He reached over and took my hand in his. "I asked you out, remember? Now, I'm not ready to end the date. Are you?"

I shook my head, my insides vibrating. "No, I'm not ready either."

"Good." Jake pulled out of the parking lot and started driving in the opposite direction of my house.

"Where are we going now?" I bounced in my seat.

"It's a surprise." He winked at me.

CHAPTER 5

Mal

THE SOFT BEAMS OF LIGHT FROM THE STREET LAMPS illuminated Jake's light brown hair, giving it a tinge of gold. His bright blue eyes lit up with joy as he began to sing, and his voice carried like bells along the night air. His fingertips tapped lightly on the steering wheel in perfect rhythm as he sang.

I fought the urge to lean over and kiss him. Aside from the fact he was driving, I could never just kiss someone. What if they weren't into it? That didn't stop me from staring at his lips. I had spent the last few years imagining what it would be like to kiss him. He had to be a great kisser. Jake dated plenty of girls over the years. I slumped in the chair. Stop thinking about that!

We pulled onto the road that led to the lake. I smiled, realizing where he was taking me. The lake was one of my favorite places. Really, any place where I could swim was perfect. I was on the swim team for years. I could have been better at it, but I had fun. My clumsiness carried over to my front stroke.

Jake parked the truck on the side of the road, and we got out, making our way down to the lake. The moon was full, casting a soft glow over the water. The sound of crickets and bullfrogs filled the air.

Jake took my hand and led me towards the water. "Remember all the times we would come here as kids," he said, his voice soft. "When I first moved here, I never thought I would like it. Then I met Frankie, Matty, and Rex. I never thought one day I would be here alone with Frankie's little sister."

"Is that a bad thing?" I asked, looking out over the water.

Jake squeezed my hand. "No, it's perfect."

My heart skipped a beat as he leaned in closer to me. His breath tickled my cheek. I closed my eyes, waiting for the kiss. But instead of pressing his lips to mine, he whispered in my ear.

"I know you like Matty and Rex," he said, his voice low. "But I want you to know that I like you too. I've liked you for a long time. Everything is complicated with us leaving. Well, I'm trying to say..."

"Look, it's them!" a voice shouted from above. Two men were making their way toward us.

I squinted into the darkness. There was no denying who was coming. Matty's tall, slender frame was silhouetted by the glow of the moon. Rex's massive, muscular body grew with each step he took towards us.

My heart fluttered. Being around all three of these men made my brain turn to mush. How did they suck the air out of my lungs by just existing?

Jake squeezed my hand. I was on a date with him. I had no right to crush on all three of them. Yet, Jake knew I did. Was I that obvious?

Matty and Rex finally reached us, both of them grinning. "So cool you guys are here!" Matty exclaimed, throwing his arms around Jake.

Rex pulled me in for a hug, his massive arms enveloping me. "Hey there, little sis," he said, ruffling my hair.

I was being torn in two different directions. On the one hand, I was enjoying spending time with Jake. On the other hand, I couldn't deny my attraction towards Matty and Rex.

I cleared my throat and kicked at the dirt. "What are you guys doing out here?"

"Just taking a walk," Matty said, looking around the area. "We were bored. Frankie is on a date, and apparently, so is Jake."

Rex smiled, "You guys wanna go for a swim?"

Jake slid his hand into mine. "Actually, we were just about to leave." He gently guided me toward the truck.

"Nonsense." Matty slapped Jake's back. "Come on."

Rex pulled his shirt off. Even in the darkness, his muscles pulsated like he had just bench-pressed a car. "Last one to the buoy loses."

My cheeks burned. There was no way I could strip down to my underwear and bra in front of them. I knew Jake, and I weren't gonna fool around tonight, so I wore a lime green bra and purple underwear. Ugh, I should have listened to Sammy when she told me to always be prepared to get naked. I looked toward the truck. I could always sit and watch as they raced.

Matty was already in his rubber ducky boxers and flexing his pecs at me. Rex bounced from one foot to the other ready to race. These boys loved their games. I didn't have to look at Jake to know he would participate.

Jake blew a kiss at me as he kicked off his sneakers and unbuttoned his jeans. Tingles ran through my body. There was no way I could do this.

"You coming?" Matty asked.

"No, I'll watch." I pointed toward the truck. "I can referee."

"You will do no such thing," Rex gasped. "If we have to strip you and toss you in the water, we will."

"Fine," I sighed.

"Good." Matty kissed me on the cheek and then ran into the water.

Butterflies erupted in my stomach as I undressed. It wasn't as if I had never gone swimming with them. But this time, we were all in our underwear and alone. This was what I wanted. I took a deep breath and expelled all doubt and nerves. I wouldn't let myself ruin this moment.

"Race you to the buoy, sweetheart." Jake winked at me with a mischievous glint, then he turned and sprinted into the water.

I laughed, the adrenaline pumping through my veins. Dashing into the water, the cool liquid washed over my skin. I swam as fast as I could, the rush of the water against my body. I could see Jake, Matty, and Rex up ahead, their arms furiously paddling through the water.

My muscles ached, but I pushed through it. I wanted them to be impressed by my swimming skills. As I got closer to them, they cheered me on. Jake was the first to reach the buoy, his arms raised triumphantly.

Matty and Rex arrived shortly after, all of them panting and laughing. I swam up to them, feeling a sense of pride that I had kept up with them.

"That was awesome!" Rex swayed back and forth as best he could in the water.

Matty nodded in agreement. "You're a pretty good swimmer, Mal. You seem to have improved since we watched your last swim meet."

I winced. "Thanks," I said, trying to brush off the compliment.

Jake wrapped his arm around me, pulling me closer. "Yeah, great job." He smiled down at me.

"Of course, you won, Jake. While some of us were studying, you were in your pool." Matty rolled his eyes. "Didn't your dad even pay for fancy swim lessons?"

"Fine, give me a different challenge," Jake replied.

"Truth or dare?" Rex smirked.

My heart quickened. Truth or dare? I knew how dangerous this game could be, especially with the three of them. They couldn't expect me to play as well. The last time they played, Frankie made snow angels in boxers, and Sammy had to ask a neighbor for shampoo while only wearing a towel.

"Sure, let's do it." Jake flicked his tongue against the roof of his mouth.

Matty rubbed his hands together eagerly. "Okay, I'll start. Rex, truth or dare?"

"Dare," Rex grinned.

Matty's eyes glistened. "I dare you to skinny dip around the buoy."

Rex laughed, "You got it." Rex pulled off his boxers and tossed them onto the buoy.

Heat rose to my cheeks as he climbed onto the buoy. Damn. His body was carved from pure stone. No wonder he was so good at football. I tried not to look at his cock, but I couldn't help it. Even flaccid, it was like him, massive. He dove into the water before they caught me gawking at him and swam around the buoy. When he finished, he winked at me. Maybe he had seen me staring.

Rex pointed to me. "Mal, truth or dare?"

I bit my lip. "Um, no."

"You have to play." Jake batted his eyes at me and stuck out his bottom lip.

"Fine, truth." This was dangerous.

Rex leaned in, his eyes locked onto mine. "Have you ever fantasized about any of us?"

My stomach turned, and my face was on fire. I couldn't

believe he had just asked me that. I looked around, trying to gauge their reactions. Jake looked unfazed, Matty looked curious, and Rex looked almost predatory.

I took a deep breath and nodded. "Yes, I have."

"Who, when, what, all of us?" Matty's eyes grew wide.

I grinned. "Nope, I already answered. Jake, truth or dare?"

His eyes locked onto mine as he said, "Dare."

I bit my lip. He was challenging me, daring me to say something dirty. I steadied my breathing. My skin vibrated. "Kiss me."

He leaned in, his lips grazing my skin. I closed my eyes. His lips traveled across my jaw to my neck. His hands gripped my waist, pulling me close. His lips found my pulse, leaving a trail of kisses up my neck. He groaned into my ear, sending a shiver down my spine.

"Wait, shit," Rex's voice came out husky. "Let's take it to my house."

Matty nodded in agreement. "Good call. This is too hard to do in the water."

I clenched my fists, trying to reign in my hormones. I had fantasized about all three of them multiple times. *Could I really do this?* Yeah, it was just truth or dare, but I knew where it was heading. My hands trembled.

"No way. The last time we played, I ended up running around the neighborhood naked." Jake shook his head.

I gasped, covering my mouth with my hands. "Oh my gosh, you didn't." I hadn't been there for that game.

The guys laughed. "He did." Matty nodded.

I shook my head, covering my mouth to hide my smile. "That's pretty funny."

"Not for me. Why don't we call it a night." Jake averted his eyes.

I looked down, hoping they couldn't see my disappointment in the glow of the moonlight. Being around all three of them was fun and easy. Jake squeezed my hand, reminding me I was on a date with him.

In truth, it didn't matter if I liked all three and all three liked me back. They were leaving. It was probably for the best because as much fun as I had with Jake, I couldn't pick just one of them.

"Let's at least race back to shore." Rex dove into the water and took off before we could reply.

I shook my head and raced after him. Matty and Jake were already closing in on him. I did my best to keep up, but all three were almost a foot taller than me. In height alone, they had the advantage.

When we reached the shore, I looked down, remembering how little I was wearing. I grabbed my clothes and quickly tossed them on, very aware of the three sets of eyes on me. Once I finished, I noticed they hadn't bothered to get dressed. They had their clothes in their hands and headed toward the vehicles.

Jake and I walked in silence, the moonlight casting a glow on our faces. He was so close that I could feel his breath on my neck. I wanted him to kiss me. I wanted him to taste my lips, to feel his body against mine.

I averted my gaze as he unlocked the door to his truck. I didn't want the night to end. My stomach turned as he drove me home.

"I had a really great time." He patted my thigh.

"Me too," I whispered.

He pulled up between my house and his. Frankie was home, shit. He was supposed to still be out on a date. If he saw me with Jake, he would flip out. Frankie never paid much attention to what I did but told me numerous times to never date his friends.

"I would walk you to your door, but your brother would fight me." Jake unclipped his seatbelt.

"Oh, I know." I grabbed the handle of the door.

Jake leaned over and pressed his lips against mine. Heat pooled between my legs, and I moaned into his mouth. His lips trailed down my neck, leaving tingles in its wake.

He pulled away and looked into my eyes, his gaze intense. "I really like you," he whispered, barely audible above the sound of crickets chirping in the night air. "I have to be honest. Matty and Rex are probably going to ask you out now. I just want you to know I don't mind."

I opened my mouth to respond, then quickly closed it. What did he mean by that? Was he giving me the okay to date all three of them?

My heart raced, and I opened my mouth to speak again, but he leaned back in for another kiss. This one was stronger than before. His hands grabbed my waist and pulled me closer until every inch of his body was against mine.

Just when things were getting heated, a light flicked on inside the house. Frankie must have heard the truck pull up! I quickly pushed Jake away, my heart racing faster than ever before.

"I better get out of here." I frantically grabbed my bag from the floor of the truck. "Please don't mention this to Frankie."

Jake nodded. I hopped out of the truck and made a beeline for home, not daring to look back.

CHAPTER 6

Matty

I DIDN'T HAVE ANY FRIENDS WHEN I WAS A KID. IT
was too hard when I kept switching classes. The first time was
when I was in first grade. The teachers made such a spectacle
of it.

Mrs. Zonny stopped in the middle of teaching with an
extraordinary announcement. She had me get up and pack up
my cubby. "This is so exciting," Mrs. Z said, her dark eyes
glinting like chips of onyx against her pale skin. All the kids
stared at me.

Suddenly, the janitor entered the room and unceremoni-
ously picked up my desk. For a moment, I was confident I was
going to be expelled. Mrs. Zonny then had us all follow the
janitor to another classroom. He placed my desk in its new
spot and told me to sit there.

The teacher of that class informed everyone I was being
moved up to a third-grade class because all my test scores were
off the charts. Instead of congratulations, the other kids
laughed and called me a nerd.

After that, I didn't bother making friends. Every time I
tried, they thought I was too young or weird to play with. In

an attempt to help me academically, my parents moved me and my little sister to a town with a fantastic school system.

I was eleven and in my freshman year of high school when we moved. Surprisingly, that day was one of the best I had in school. No one bothered me or even questioned why I was there. Later, I discovered I wasn't the first kid genius there, and the principal had strict rules against bullying. I triumphantly got off the bus and headed down the street toward my house when a boy with clothes too big and a massive overbite came running over to me.

"That's the wrong bus," he said. "How did you get home from the high school bus?"

"I'm in high school." I pulled the straps on my bookbag tighter.

"No way. How old are you?" he asked as he stared at my face gauging my age.

"Eleven. My name is Matty Chen." I stuck out my hand.

"Cool, I'm Frankie." He slapped my hand. "That little girl running toward us is my little sis, Mal. Let's hide from her. She is so annoying."

"I don't mind. She can hang with us." I shrugged. I knew all about being bullied and being left out. This little girl with lopsided pigtails shouldn't feel that way.

"Come on. She just wants to be around me and my best friend, Jake. She will annoy you within five minutes." Frankie crossed his arms.

"Bet." I stuck out my hand.

"Huh?" The kid scratched his chin.

"Two dollars. She annoys me within five minutes, and I pay. She doesn't, and you pay." I kept my hand stuck out.

Frankie shook my hand just as the little girl approached us. She bent over and sucked in as much breath as her little lungs could handle.

"Hey, I'm Mal. Why is your bookbag so big?" She pointed at me.

"I'm Matty. I go to high school. Wanna play a game?" I smiled down at her.

"Sure. What kind? I love games." She stood upright.

"It's called hush." I pulled a dollar bill from my pocket. "You hang out with us without saying a word for five minutes, and I'll give you this."

She nodded and made a zipper motion across her lips. Five minutes later and Frankie paid up. I was up a dollar and proved to the new kid that his sister didn't have to be considered annoying. After that, I always convinced Frankie to let Mal hang with us. I wasn't sure why but eleven-year-old me knew Mal was the only girl for me.

As she grew up and became the kind, clumsy girl that laughed wholeheartedly, I knew the younger me was correct. No other girl in the world compared to her.

"I can't believe you guys are all leaving at the end of summer." Frankie clicked on the TV.

"I was just thinking about how we met. If it wasn't for you, I would still be the weird kid that studies too much." I grabbed the controller and started up Last of Us.

"You still are the weird kid. Just think about all the fun you would have missed out on." Frankie punched me in the arm.

I shoved him back. "I'm going to get you for that. Now tell me about this new girl you have been seeing. Is she as hot as you say?"

He leaned back against the couch, my feet propped on the coffee table. "She is fucking hot, man. I can't stop thinking about her."

"Nice, when do I meet her?" I asked.

"Soon, what about you? You talking to anyone?"

Images of Mal filled my mind. I couldn't help but think of Mal, but my heart was heavy with guilt. She was the perfect woman — beautiful, intelligent, witty, and just the right amount of quirkiness. But she was Frankie's little sister, and Rex and Jake clearly had feelings for her too. Not that that bothered me. Even though I wanted to pursue things, a part of me knew it would be wrong because of Frankie.

As if she heard my thoughts, Mal walked into the room. Mal plopped on the sofa next to us and drank a sip of my soda. I smiled at her and turned my attention back to the video game.

"Mal, go away." Frankie rolled his eyes.

"Stop being a dick. Have you heard from Dad? This weekend is the anniversary, and I thought he would be home for it. Not that I care." Mal clicked away at her phone, not looking at either of us.

I knew the anniversary they talked about. The death of their mother. She died of cancer a few years ago at the age of forty-seven. The two siblings had been really close to their mom.

"I've texted him, no response," Frankie said. "You think he has another woman stashed away somewhere?"

"That's disgusting. Stop being an asshole." Mal widened her emerald eyes at Frankie.

"I have an idea," I said. "Why don't we all go somewhere for the weekend? We can take my car."

"I don't know about that," Mal said.

"I'm in," Frankie said. "Ya know what. I can rent a lake house. Get a bunch of us to go. It'll be great."

"You aren't gonna be able to do that last minute. Plus, there is no way I'll get off from work." Mal crossed her arms.

"I know a guy. Plus, all the money I make from throwing parties. It'll be great. Besides, you don't have to go, Mal."

Frankie picked up his phone and started texting. He always knew a guy. I had no doubt we would have a fantastic place on the lake to spend the weekend.

"Why don't you ask about getting someone to cover for you. You could even see if Sammy wants to go." I wanted her to be there. Even if nothing happened between us, seeing her in a bikini would be worth it.

Mal's cheeks flushed red. "I don't think that's a good idea. I know Frankie doesn't want his little sis bothering him."

Frankie raised an eyebrow. "Oh, stop being a brat. You can go. Just don't annoy me."

Mal dropped her head. "I'll think about it."

I wanted to insist she join us, but I knew that would look suspicious. Instead, I turned to Frankie. "So when are we leaving?"

"This Friday," he said. "I already booked the lake house."

I couldn't wait for the weekend to arrive. It would be the perfect opportunity to spend time with Mal and sort out my feelings for her. That was if she even went.

Mal got up and walked out of the room. I was curious to know if she wanted to come. So much of me wanted to follow her and tell her I wanted her to be there with us. Instead, I stayed on the sofa and continued the game.

After a while, Frankie got off his phone and turned to me. "Okay, Rex and Jake are in. So are about ten other people. It's gonna be a blast."

"Yeah, for sure." My stomach twisted. "It's not my place, but you should make Mal feel more welcome."

"No way. Look, she has a crush on you, Rex, and Jake. I'm not gonna make her feel welcome." He took a chug of his soda. "Don't look at me like that. She'll still go. This way, she doesn't think we want her hanging around us. Sammy and her will do whatever it is they do the whole time. And if Sammy can't make it, Mal will stay by the water reading books the whole time."

I decided to take matters into my own hands and went to find Mal. I found her sitting outside on the front porch, reading.

"Hey," I said, taking a seat next to her. "Mind if I join you?"

She shrugged. "Sure."

I rubbed my hands together and stared at the front lawn. "You know your brother actually wants you with us this weekend."

Mal looked up from her book. "Doubtful. It's cool. I got work. It's not a big deal."

I could see that she was trying to hide her disappointment, so I decided to take a chance and speak my mind. "I really hope you change your mind. It wouldn't be the same without you."

A smile tugged at the corner of her lips. "Thanks, Matty. I appreciate it, but don't want to be a burden."

I shook my head. "You're not a burden. You're part of the group, and we want you there."

She looked at me, searching my eyes for any sign of insincerity. After a moment, she smiled again. "I'll think about it."

I didn't want to push her too hard, but I also didn't want her to miss out on what could be a fun time. "Mal, it'll be a great weekend. You can relax by the lake, read your books, and enjoy the company of friends. And who knows, maybe we'll play more truth or dare."

Her face turned beat red. She stared at me for a full minute before returning to her book. I wasn't sure if she was excited at the thought or mortified.

I decided to change the subject before it got too awkward. "So, what are you reading?"

She showed me the cover. "It's called 'Unhinged Witch' by Melody Caraballo. It's really good."

"I've never heard of it," I admitted.

"That makes sense. It's paranormal romance. There is this talking cat, and she is so funny. She loves meatballs."

I couldn't help but smile. She was always surprising me. "Maybe you can recommend some more books for me to read."

"I would love to," she said, her eyes lighting up. "I have a whole list of recommendations for you."

"You could bring them to our date tomorrow." I cleared my throat and stared at my feet.

"Huh?" She dropped her book.

"A date. If you want." I shuffled my feet. "You can swing by my house, and I can cook."

"Okay," Mal whispered.

"Cool." I picked up her book and handed it to her. Before she had a chance to change her mind, I took off.

CHAPTER 7

Mal

I WALKED BY THE HOSTESS WITH BUTTERFLIES IN MY stomach. I was heading to Matty's house as soon as I was done. He planned on cooking for me and wouldn't tell me what it was. Not that I minded. I was just excited to be around him.

"Are you leaving early?" Paula, the hostess, snapped at me.

"No. Sammy is just covering my side work." I stopped in my tracks, almost dropping my tray of food. "Why? Is everything okay?"

"Sure. You have to explain to Barbara why you left early, not me." Paula smacked her gum at me.

"We cover for each other all the time," I gasped. "I'm not even leaving yet. I'm finishing my tables."

"Whatever." Paula grabbed a few menus as a couple walked through the door. "I have work to do."

I ground my teeth and walked over to my table. The little boy sitting there practically jumped out of his seat when he saw the chicken fingers. I didn't blame the kid. They were delicious. I set the food down and walked away, still shaking my head at how rude the hostess was. She had never liked me, and I couldn't figure out why. It's not like I was popular and expected everyone to like me, but I never did anything to her.

We even went to school together. Last year when I started working with her, she seemed friendly. She had even brought up how I was in her calculus class. I mentioned to her how bad my grades were, and if it wasn't for Matty tutoring me, I would have failed. She seemed to praise Matty for being so self-less and then never spoke to me again.

Sammy thought it was all in my head, and that Paula was really friendly. Maybe Sammy was right, but it didn't appear that way. On the day's Paula was working, I got crappy tables, double sat, and other times skipped in the rotation. Since I couldn't prove she was actually doing it on purpose, I never brought it up to Barbara.

"Why the sad face?" Sammy tapped my shoulder. "I'm doing your side work."

"Oh, it's nothing." I smiled faintly at her. "I know you are, and I really appreciate it."

"I don't mind as long as I get all the details of you and Matty." Sammy scooped ice into a glass.

"You know if anything happens, I'm not telling you." I set down my tray and leaned against the wall.

"Come on. You have three hot, hunky, delicious guys after you, and you are gonna leave me in the dark?" Sammy filled the cup with soda and set it on her tray.

"I wouldn't say after me. I'm not sure what I would say. I'm just closing my eyes and hoping this never ends because whatever it is with them is intoxicating." I smiled and crossed my arms. It really was terrific.

"Oh, they are after you. I can tell just by the smile you have on your face." Sammy pursed her lips. "Look, I got closing tonight anyway. Go. I'll finish up your tables. Shower, shave your vagina, and put on something sexy. Maybe Rex and Jake will stop by, and you can lose your virginity to all three."

"Sammy!" I snapped. "You can't say things like that."

"Why not?" She scrunched up her face.

"People might hear you," I whispered. The waitress station was just a short distance from the tables. One of the customers could have been eaves-dropping.

"Are you worried about them knowing you're a virgin or that you want three men?" Sammy asked.

"Both," I hissed. My sex life, or lack thereof, was no one's business.

"Okay, I'm sorry. Go home, get ready for your date. Think of it as my apology." Sammy walked off, knowing I would accept.

I tipped out the busboys and Paula. She politely informed me that Barbara would absolutely be hearing about me leaving early. To ensure I would still have a job, I texted Barbara and let her know what happened. As I started my car, she replied that it was fine as long as I had coverage.

A few minutes later, I pulled up to my house. The first thing I did was look for Jake's truck in his driveway. It wasn't there, but his mom's car was. I wanted to tell her how much I enjoyed Gloria's but decided not to because she may not have known that Jake and I had gone on a date. She was always kind to me, but she may not have liked the idea of me going out with Jake. So instead of knocking on her door, I went inside my house.

My father charged at me and pulled me into a hug. I stood lifeless as he swung me back and forth. I hadn't expected him to be home. Even when he was supposed to be home, he barely ever was. When he finally released me, I gave him a quick half-smile and started up the stairs.

"That's it?" my dad's voice screeched as he spoke. "I haven't been home in weeks, and I get a forced smile."

"Uh, I'm in a rush." I shrugged.

"A rush? I was hoping we could go grab a bite or watch a

movie. We barely get to spend time together, and I would love to catch you up on everything in my life." He grabbed the bottom railing and looked up at me with big pleading eyes.

"Can't. Maybe tomorrow. At least you will be home for this weekend." I chewed the inside of my lip.

"I gotta go back to work tomorrow night." He checked his watch.

"Oh." I wanted to scream at him. He could have changed his plans to be home with us. Instead of doing any of that, I averted the attention. "Why don't you ask Frankie to hang out tonight?"

"I already said no." Frankie walked out of the kitchen toward the front door. "I'm meeting Jake and Rex at the basketball courts."

"Why so late? And why no Matty?" I asked, my voice was way too high-pitched.

"Matty said he had plans. The courts have lights, and we are gonna hustle some high schoolers out of money," Frankie chuckled. "They think they are better than us. Rex is literally a multi-sport athlete. There isn't anything he can't play."

"But he is no Bo Jackson." My dad pointed at Frankie. That man always had to make sure everyone knew there was someone better than them in the world. I once said I wanted to be a dancer. He said I would never be a Maddie Ziegler. Frankie said he wanted to be a sports broadcaster. My dad let him know he would never be an Al Michaels. So as we got older, we stopped telling him our dreams.

"Well, on that delightful piece of news, I gotta go." Frankie nodded and walked out the door.

I rushed up the stairs and into my bedroom before my dad tried to make me feel guilty for going out instead of spending time with him. He was always like that, big guilt trips, and then he would leave early in the morning before Frankie and I got up. Ever since my mom passed away, my dad buried himself in his work and left Frankie to raise me. For the longest, I felt terrible for my dad. That was until Sammy made a very keen observation, he wasn't the only one to lose someone. Frankie and I lost our mom, and he gave no sort of comfort to us.

Pushing aside any more dark thoughts that would ruin the evening, I went to the closet and stared at the mess inside. After the date with Jake, I shoved all my clothes to the bottom and figured I would clean it up later. I didn't expect to have a date with Matty two days later.

Shit. What was I going to wear? I got on my hands and knees and started digging for something that wasn't wrinkled and would look nice. The date was just at Matty's house, so I didn't have to worry about dressing up, but I still wanted to look nice for him. I pulled out my phone.

SAMMY

> What am I supposed to wear?

Nothing. Go naked.

> Please.

Jeans and a black tank top. Simple yet sexy. Oh, and wear socks and sneakers. You want to avoid going to his house, taking off your sandals, and walking barefoot.

> Um, okay. Thanks.

Even though I wasn't sure why it would matter if I was barefoot or not, I took her advice. Sammy knew way more about guys than I did. It wasn't just about her experience with them. She could get them to do just about anything. During freshman year of high school, we all piled into the auditorium for some speaker about drug prevention. The entire school was forced to attend. When we were going to our seats, Sammy let me in the aisle first and just so happened to end up next to a really hunky senior. When we got up to leave, Sammy was wearing the guy's sweater. When I asked her how she did it, she replied, 'Witch magic.' I knew the truth. She had a way with men.

I showered and shaved everything. Not that Matty would be getting any action tonight, but there was no harm in being prepared. If I had any underwear that was provocative in the least bit, I would have considered wearing them. I didn't. So, I opted for a flowery pair with a non-matching navy bra.

Sammy had given me so much extra time that I sat on my bed staring at the ceiling. Seriously, who thought popcorn ceilings were a good look? I checked my phone every few minutes to see if it was time to leave yet. Time was going backward.

Finally, after what must have been an eternity, I tied up my sneakers and headed for the door. I expected my dad to bombard me again and remind me that I should be spending time with him and him alone. He didn't, so I left the house and started the car. One last glance at Jake's house let me know my dad was standing on the porch bothering Jake's mom. She was too kind to tell him to go away. Since I was grateful for the distraction, I didn't try to save her from him. Instead, I took off down the street to Matty's.

He only lived a block away; technically, I could have walked there. It would be obvious if I did. Sammy didn't live far, and I always drove to her house, so I wanted Frankie and my dad to assume I went there.

I parked in front of Matty's house and turned off the engine. Taking a deep breath, I flipped down the visor and gave myself one last look in the mirror. My make-up could have been better, but I didn't do a horrible job. The eyeshadow and lipstick were in the correct place, and really, that was all that mattered.

My door flung open.

"Ah!" I screamed.

"Sorry, I didn't mean to startle you," Matty chuckled. "You know I wanted to pick you up."

"I almost got caught with Jake dropping me off. I didn't want to take any chances." I grabbed my purse and stepped out of the car. "Sorry, I shouldn't have brought that up." What was the proper etiquette for dating two guys?

"Bring him up all you want. Honestly, I think it's hot that you went on a date with him and now me." Matty shut my car door and walked me to his house.

Heat rushed to my face. "Oh, cool. Um, so where are your parents and sister?"

"Yale. Evie got an early acceptance, so they went to check it out." Matty led me inside.

Candles littered the floor, and soft music filled the air. A table with two settings and even more candles was set up in the dining room. Even though it was summertime, he had the fireplace going. It didn't pour out heat, so I assumed it was only for aesthetic purposes. On the table was also a bouquet of sunflowers, my favorite.

"Wow, Matty, this is gorgeous." I held my hand to my chest.

"This is nothing. I had planned on using Rex's place since he had plans tonight, but since my parents are out of town, I figured this would work." Matty shoved his hands in his pockets.

Rex was the only one to have his own place. He had a bad relationship with his parents, and he was gone the day he turned eighteen. Jake, Matty, and Frankie had planned on moving in with him one day, but they all had their own reasons not to. Jake didn't want to leave his mom alone,

Frankie didn't want to leave me alone, and Matty had over-bearing, strict parents that he didn't want to disappoint. Even with that, I knew all three helped Rex pay the bills, so he never had to go crawling back home.

"Wait, did you say Yale?" I asked.

"Yeah. Evie is considering forgoing her senior year and attending." Matty shrugged.

"Forgoing? She is thirteen." I had to practically force my mouth shut. The Chens were all incredibly intelligent. I was pretty sure it was a mix of genes and strict parenting.

"Yeah. My parents are considering moving to Connecticut to watch out for her. Since I'll be moving, they don't need to stay here." Matty pulled out a chair for me to sit down.

"They really are all about education." I drove the conversation away for talk of him moving.

"Well, my parents grew up poor. My dad had to drop out of school when he was fourteen to start working. He didn't want that for us. It just so happened they got lucky with two genius kids." Matty flashed his teeth at me. "I'll be right back."

A few moments later, Matty returned to the dining room carrying a tray filled with food. There was asparagus, wet rice, shrimp, and something that looked like meat inside bread. The smells intoxicated my sense and made my mouth water.

"What is all that?" I asked.

"This is mushroom risotto." He pointed to the wet rice. "This is beef Wellington. I cooked it on the medium well side. I know you don't like your steak bloody. Oh, and then a simple shrimp cocktail and some asparagus. Don't worry. There are no carrots."

"Wow, Matty. This is the fanciest meal I have ever seen. How did you learn to cook like this?" I knew he could cook, but this was next-level food.

"I love cooking. My mom taught me some, and the rest I

51

learned from online videos." He dished out the food onto both of our plates.

"Why didn't you become a chef instead of a professor?" I clenched my hands to prevent myself from diving in before he sat down.

"My parents sacrificed everything for me. They would be heartbroken." Matty took a napkin, unfolded it, and placed it in my lap. Then he sat down and did the same.

"Thank you for this." I took a bite of the risotto. It literally melted in my mouth.

Bite after bite, I devoured everything. I couldn't believe I wasn't at a restaurant. It was easily one of my all-time favorite meals. Matty could have become a five-star chef with his own restaurant.

I stopped to take a drink of my water. Matty was sitting across from me, hands clasped, staring at me. I averted my eyes and continued to drink.

"Would you like seconds?" he asked.

"No, thank you. I'm stuffed. This was incredible. I don't know how to thank you." I was rambling, and I couldn't stop. "I think that's the right thing to say. I just mean. Wow, Matty. You are like a serious super chef."

"Ha. ha. Thank me by coming to the lake house." He raised his eyebrows at me.

"Fine," I smirked. "How come you barely touched your food?"

"Uh. Sampling food while cooking can really fill you up." He pushed his plate away. "So, you wanna watch a movie? Or play a game?"

"A movie works."

Five minutes later, we were on the sofa with a movie playing. Matty and I talked through the entire thing. We avoided touchy subjects like, his parents and the future. He cracked jokes the whole time and brought up truth or dare. I laughed it off even though I was intrigued by the thought.

Once the movie ended, he just hit replay since neither one of us paid any attention to it. I yawned a few times and ignored how tired I was since I wasn't ready to end our night. At one point, he wrapped his arm around me and pulled me into him. I nuzzled in and drifted off to sleep.

CHAPTER 8

Mal

TOWN DINER WAS OVERRUN WITH CUSTOMERS. FOR a Wednesday night, it shouldn't have been so busy. Barb, the manager, only put Sammy and me on for the night. It was way more than either of us could handle.

By seven, my feet were sore, and I wasn't sure if I had given the last table lemons with their water. Sammy complained about how frantic it was, but I couldn't listen. All I could think about was this weekend and whether I should go. I had told Matty I would, but I debated backing out.

"Hey, are you even listening?" Sammy snapped her fingers in my face.

I shook my head, trying to focus. "Sorry, what?"

"I said, do you wanna come by my house after this?" she asked.

I nodded. "Yeah, that sounds good."

The rest of the night was a blur, but somehow we closed the restaurant in record time. We drove over to her house. I hadn't told her much about what had happened the last few days. I wasn't sure how to bring it up. Talking about boys was always her territory. She knew the basics but not the details.

"So, what's been going on lately?" Sammy asked, pouring a glass of water for each of us.

I shrugged. "I don't know. It's just. Uh."

"Okay, something is up. Spill."

"Where do I begin?" I took a sip. Tonight was so busy at work I hadn't had the chance to drink anything.

"How about the date with Jake? Did you blow him?" I nearly spit out my water, almost choking on it. "What? No! Sammy, come on."

Sammy laughed. "Relax, I'm just kidding. But seriously, how did it go?"

"It was amazing. We went to a fancy restaurant. He opened doors for me. Um. And we wenttothelakewhereiplayedtruthordarewithJakeMattyandRex."

Sammy spit out her drink. "Could you say that again?"

"You heard. And before you ask, no, nothing crazy happened. We stopped playing. Then yesterday, I had my date with Matty, and he tried convincing me to go to the lake house."

"You really need to give me more context. What lake house?"

I took a deep breath. "Well, Frankie rented a place for the weekend. All the guys are gonna be there."

Sammy's eyes widened. "And?"

"And," I hesitated, "I don't know if I should go. I mean, it's not like I'm really a part of the group or anything."

Sammy rolled her eyes. "Mal, you're always invited. You're Frankie's sister. Plus, you're pretty much best friends with all of them now and potentially dating all of them. Not to mention, I bought a new bathing suit that needs an excuse to be worn."

I laughed at her shopping habits. The girl knew how to spend money. "Yeah, but I don't know. I don't want to be a burden or anything."

Sammy shook her head. "You're not going to be a burden. Look, we will go. It'll be great."

I nodded, feeling a little better about the idea of going. "Okay, I'll think about it."

Sammy grinned. "Good. Now, let's talk about something else. Have you been reading anything interesting lately?"

I smiled, grateful for the change in topic. "Actually, I just started reading 'Unhinged Witch' by Melody Caraballo. It's really interesting so far."

Sammy's eyes lit up. "Oh, I love that book! It's so spicy. Have you read any other books by her?"

I shook my head. "No, this is my first one. But I'm definitely going to check out more of her work."

We spent the rest of the night discussing books, movies, and our possible plans for the weekend. By the time I got home, I was exhausted.

I woke up early and got ready to head out. Before I made a final decision, there was someone I wanted to visit. There were only a few hours before my shift. Barb really had me on the schedule a lot this week. That wasn't a complaint. I needed the money.

Frankie tried to stop me on the way out the door. I didn't feel like talking to him. Every year around the anniversary, my presence made him edgy and even more bothersome. As far as older brothers went, he was great when necessary.

When I was twelve, a boy at school, Dan West, kept picking on me. My parents said that was how boys act when they really liked you. I thought it was bullshit. If someone liked you, they shouldn't call you 'book girl' and knock all your books out of your hands every chance they got.

In a fit of tears, I told Frankie. He skipped school that day, along with Jake, Matty, and Rex. They made the kid piss himself. That was six years ago, and every time I passed Dan on the streets, he put his head down and went in the opposite direction.

Just because Frankie had his moments didn't mean he didn't make me angry. He shouldn't even attempt to be okay with leaving me alone during the anniversary. I ground my teeth and started the car.

After stopping at the grocery store for flowers, I headed to see my mom. Maybe she would have answers for me. I drove up close to her plot, and walked over to her headstone.

I kneeled down and placed the flowers in front of her gravestone. "Hey, Mom. It's been a while since I've visited. Things have been crazy lately."

I took a deep breath, trying to steady my emotions. "I don't know what to do about the lake house. The guys invited me, but I don't want to be a burden. And it's been hard lately, with the anniversary of your death coming up. Well, I need your advice. I don't know if I should go with the guys this weekend. I'm scared, Mom. Scared of what might happen. Scared of what might not happen. I don't know if I'm ready."

Tears started to well up in my eyes. "I wish you were here. You always knew what to say. I just feel like I'm lost without you."

A gust of wind blew past me, rustling the leaves on the trees. It was almost as if she told me she was always there, even if I couldn't see her.

I sat there for a while longer, talking to my mom about everything that had been going on. It was like a weight had been lifted off my shoulders. When I finally got up to leave, a person a few headstones away was sitting in the grass. I recognized the silhouette of his side view, Rex Wilson.

I hesitated for a moment, wondering if I should go up to

him or not. But then, I figured he could use the company. So, I took a deep breath and walked towards him.

Three years ago, Rex's oldest brother took his own life. I never asked why. It didn't matter. It happened during Rex's senior year as a starting linebacker. Rex got injured shortly after, tore a ligament in his knee.

"Hey," I said softly, trying not to startle him.

Rex turned his head to look at me. "Hey," he replied, his voice barely above a whisper.

I sat next to him and squeezed his hand. The leaves rustled again, blowing across the cemetery.

"The night before he died, he came into my room. He gave me his class ring and told me I would make it to the pros one day." He twisted the gold ring on his hand. "I should have known. Did you know that when people are ready to take their life, they give away their possessions?"

I shook my head. "No, I didn't know that."

Rex sighed heavily. "Neither did I. I just wish I could have done something to stop him."

I didn't know what to say. What could I say? There was nothing that could bring his brother back. No words could ease his pain. I rubbed his back in comforting circles, hoping it could provide some small solace.

We sat there in silence for a while, the wind blowing the leaves around us. It was peaceful, in a melancholic kind of way.

After a while, Rex stood up and brushed the grass off his pants. "Thanks for sitting with me, Mal."

"Anytime, Rex," I replied, standing up as well.

"I'll see you at the lake house, right?"

I hesitated. "I'm not sure. I have to work."

"Don't do that." He grabbed my hands.

"Do what?" I chewed my lip.

"Make excuses. You should come. It'll be fun, I promise." He gave me a small smile.

I nodded, feeling a little more convinced. "Okay, I'll see about getting the time off."

Rex's smile widened. "Great. See you there."

As he walked away, I couldn't help but be a little relieved. Going with the group wouldn't be so bad. And maybe, just maybe, it would be the distraction I needed from the weight of the anniversary looming over me.

I returned to my car and drove to work, feeling a little lighter than before. Maybe everything would work out okay in the end.

As I got out of the car, I rehearsed, asking for the weekend off. It was short notice, and Barb would probably say no. But I had to try. I straightened my shoulders and walked into the restaurant.

"Hey, Mal. You're early," Barb said, looking up from her paperwork.

"Yeah, I wanted to talk to you about something," I said, trying to sound confident.

Barb raised an eyebrow. "Go ahead."

"I was wondering if there was any way I could get this weekend off," I said, my voice hopeful.

Barb sighed. "Mal, did you even look at the schedule?"

"No, I'm sure we are short-handed, but please," I pleaded with her.

Barb looked at me for a long moment, then smiled. "Did you really think I would schedule you this weekend of all weekends? Did you not wonder why you were on the schedule so much this week?"

"Huh?"

"Good thing you are going into doing hair because you are no rocket scientist." She set her glasses on her desk. "I was good friends with your mom. So I didn't put you on this weekend.

As an extra bonus, I gave your sidekick the weekend off as well."

I smiled in relief. "Thank you, Barb. Thank you, thank you."

"Try and live a little this weekend. Don't hold up in your room reading." She went back to her paperwork.

CHAPTER 9

Mal

I COULDN'T BELIEVE MY LUCK. BARB HAD GIVEN ME the weekend off, and I was free to spend time with the guys. I couldn't wait to escape the city and spend some time in the fresh air.

As I drove home, I couldn't stop the butterflies in my stomach. I would be with Jake, Matty, and Rex for the entire weekend. My mind drifted to the other day with them. Would we really all play truth or dare, or would I have to choose between them? Ugh, how self-centered was I? It wasn't like they would stand there and say, 'Hey, Mal, take your pick.'

When I got home, I started packing my bag. I didn't need much, just a change of clothes, toiletries, and three or four books. I was never really one for outdoor activities, so I knew I would need some entertainment. So, I picked out my favorite books and quickly tossed them in my bag.

As I was packing, I heard a knock on the door. I wasn't expecting anyone, so I cautiously approached the front door.

When I opened it, it surprised me to see Jake standing there with his hands in his pockets.

"Hey, Mal. Rex told me you decided to go. Ready for the weekend?" he asked, grinning.

I smiled back at him. "Yeah, just finishing up packing. How did you know I got the time off?"

"Sammy texted me. She wanted to know if any hot single guys would be there. Excluding me, Rex, and Matty. She made it very clear she had no interest in us." Jake laughed and walked into the living room.

I shook my head. "That sounds like her."

Frankie stepped into the living room. "Hey Jake, I didn't know you were coming by."

Jake's eyes shifted from mine to Frankie's. "Uh, yeah. I figured you and I could do last-minute details. Ya know, who is riding with who, food, sleeping arrangements."

Frankie nodded. "Yeah, that sounds good. Let's go into the dining room to discuss it."

I watched them walk away, wishing it wouldn't be so awkward if I went with them. I knew I couldn't. Frankie would have a fit. He always got annoyed with me.

I finished packing my bag and walked into the dining room, where Jake and Frankie were deep in discussion. They looked up as I entered.

"Hey, Mal," Jake said with a smile.

"Hey," I replied, chewing my lip.

"Okay, so we've got the food covered. We can stop at the grocery store on the way there," Frankie said, clicking on his laptop.

"I can drive my truck," Jake offered. "It's big enough to fit all our stuff."

Frankie nodded. "That works. And we'll take my car as well."

"Sounds good." I grabbed a bottle of water to stop myself from chewing off the inside of my lip.

"Mal, you can ride with me." Jake flashed me a grin.

Heat rose to my cheeks. "Okay, sure."

We went over some more details, and then Jake left.

"Don't get any ideas." Frankie pointed a finger at me.

"Excuse me?" I gasped.

"Jake is off limits. So are Rex and Matty, for that matter." He closed his laptop.

"No, shit." I rolled my eyes. Frankie had told me that multiple times.

"Just making sure you know the rules." Frankie stood up and stretched. "Are you excited about the weekend?"

I nodded and shrugged. I didn't want him to get the idea that I was overly excited and risk him uninviting me. "Yeah, I think it'll be fun."

"Good, because we're gonna have a blast." Frankie grinned at me. "Now, let's grab some dinner before we finish packing."

We stepped into the kitchen, the smell of spices and herbs adding warmth to the room. I started chopping vegetables for the stir-fry while Frankie grabbed drinks from the fridge. As I sprinkled garlic over the pan, my heart raced as I remembered that I'd be sharing a place with the guys all weekend.

"Do you want carrots in yours?" I tossed the water chestnuts in the pan.

"And risk any getting on your plate?" Frankie scoffed. "I don't feel like taking you to the hospital tonight."

I shrugged and continued adding veggies. I was cautious about keeping carrots away from my food. One trip to the E.R. when I was seven, was all I needed to learn that lesson.

After dinner, we finished packing and headed to bed early. We had an early morning start and needed to be well-rested.

As I laid in bed, I stared at the ceiling. How was I supposed to fall asleep? I rolled over and grabbed my phone.

SAMMY

> Maybe this is a bad idea.

> Stop your shit.

> I'm serious. Even if anything happened with them, Frankie would kill me if he found out.

> Fuck him. Does he ask your permission before fucking someone? No, because he is an adult, and so are you.

> He isn't trying to hook up with my best friend.

> You should be looking up porn and learning what to do. I gotta go to bed. I gotta get up early and get my vagina waxed before we leave.

> You are too much.

> You could come with me. Get your kitty all smooth.

> I would rather use a razor. Goodnight.

> Goodnight.

I set the phone down, and it buzzed again.

JAKE

> I hope I get to have my lips on you again.

I sighed. I wanted to text him back, but I had no idea what to say. How would I reply to that without sounding like an idiot? Instead, I closed my eyes and replayed our kiss in his truck.

My hands wandered down my body. I could still taste his

tongue. His touch sent shivers down my spine. I wanted him. I wanted him so bad.

My hands moved up my shirt, caressing my breasts. Imagining Jake's hands on me, I pinched my nipples lightly. I wanted Jake to suck on my nipples. While I continued to tease myself, I bit my lip. My other hand moved down my pants and found my wet pussy.

My fingers slid down my panties and found my clit. Rubbing it softly, teasing me. I imagined Jake's tongue on my pussy. I would make him use his tongue to tease me. Then I would scream his name as he licked me.

Moaning softly as I rubbed my clit a little harder. I imagined Jake going down on me. I wanted him to stop teasing me and make me cum. Shit, I wanted him to fuck me and cum on me. Soon, Matty and Rex entered my visions. I rubbed harder, imagining all three of them tending to my needs. They would fuck me all night. They would make me cum over and over again.

I pictured them licking me, sucking my nipples, and fucking me. I was so soaked in my pussy juices that I couldn't take it anymore. Biting my lip, I tried to hold back my moans as I rubbed myself faster and harder until I came. I moaned as my hand brought me to my climax. I kept playing with my pussy until the last waves of pleasure left me.

I wasn't surprised I didn't picture just Jake for the entire fantasy. I had a crush on all three of them, and if I had it my way, I would be with all of them. Even if it was only for the summer.

CHAPTER 10

Mal

"ARE YOU READY?" FRANKIE BANGED ON MY DOOR.

"The sun isn't even up yet!" I yelled from under my covers.

"Get up, Sleeping Beauty, we have a long ride ahead of us, and we still need to stop at the grocery store."

I groaned as I buried my head under the pillow.

"Fine, I'll grab you a cup of coffee." Frankie left the room, and I heard his footsteps head toward the living room.

"Ugh, now I'm awake," I muttered as I got out of bed.

I pulled out a pair of jeans and a tank top. I didn't even bother showering. I walked into the kitchen and took the cup of coffee Frankie handed me.

Jake walked into the kitchen and poured himself some. He smiled at me and kept glancing at my chest. I looked down, confused, and realized I was so tired I didn't put on a bra.

Heat rose to my cheeks as I turned and left to fix myself. As I was in my room getting ready, Sammy walked in. Seriously, no one ever knocked.

"I am so ready for this!" Sammy tossed her arms in the air. "I texted Jake last night, and he said Billy was coming. You know, the guy Frankie always gets to bounce at his parties. The guy has seriously large muscles and probably a large..."

"Anyway. We gotta hurry up." I cut her off. "Frankie wants to stop and get groceries on the way there."

I grabbed my bags and headed downstairs. Matty and Rex also showed up. They both smiled at me when I entered the living room. Yeah, this is gonna be a long weekend.

"Let's go." Frankie clapped his hands together.

"Isn't your girl riding with us?" Matty asked Frankie.

"Uh, no. She is meeting us there. She is grabbing the alcohol, so we don't have to stop for that as well." Frankie grabbed his bag and headed outside.

"Does she have a name?" I asked.

"Yup."

I rolled my eyes and followed him outside. Matty, Rex, and Sammy tossed their stuff in Frankie's car.

"Shit, I forgot my bathing suit. I guess I'll be skinny dipping." Sammy shrugged.

Frankie turned around. "Sammy!"

"What? I'm going to skinny dip." She hopped in the back seat of his car.

"Not in front of everybody," Frankie shook his head. Sammy rolled her eyes, and then she and Frankie exchanged a look. Frankie shook his head and got in the driver's seat.

"That was odd." I hopped in the truck with Jake.

"Not really. You know how Sammy is. I'm sure he is just looking out for her." He started the truck and followed Frankie.

When we got to the lake house, I was impressed. Frankie had really outdone himself. The house was beautiful, with a large deck that looked out onto the lake. Inside were seven bedrooms, a kitchen with stainless steel appliances, and a vast living room with a fireplace.

I had expected us to be at the lake I was at the other day with Jake. Instead, this place was two hours away. Lake Gem was ten times the size of the one near my house. This had many homes around it, and so many people were already on the water in boats and jet skis.

"Frankie, this is amazing," I gasped.

"I do side work for the guy who owns this." He set down his bag.

"So, which room is mine?" I had gotten up so early. I wanted to lay down for a bit.

"You and Sammy are together upstairs. Pick any room. I have the master downstairs. Matty and Rex are sharing, and Jake and Billy have another one," Frankie replied.

"I thought you said like ten other people are coming?" I asked. This house was big, but I didn't think it would fit everyone.

"Only four more. Harry and Donnie, my buddies from college, and they are bringing two of their friends." Frankie counted on his fingers. "Yeah, that's it. I was gonna invite more, but then the house gets crowded. Besides, twelve people are more than enough."

"They are bringing their girlfriends? Damn, like everyone is gonna be paired up." Sammy tossed her hand on her hip.

"They are dating each other, so no girlfriends for them." Frankie shook his head as if this was common knowledge. I knew it because I had met them plenty of times, but Sammy hadn't.

"Well, I'm going to take a nap." I grabbed my bag and headed upstairs.

"I'm gonna help them unpack." Sammy handed me her bag to bring up as well.

. . .

A few hours later, I woke up to laughter downstairs. I brushed my teeth and pulled my jeans back on. I headed downstairs to find a beautiful woman with long black hair and dark eyes standing in the kitchen. A wonderful aroma of herbs and spices filled the air.

"Hi, I'm Rachel." She waved a spatula at me.

"I'm Mal." I sat down at the kitchen island.

"Oh." She dropped the spatula and clapped her hands together. "You're Frankie's sister. Wow. Hi. I'm his girlfriend. He said you weren't coming this weekend. I'm so happy I get to meet you."

"Yeah, same." I chewed my lip. "So, where is everyone?"

"Outside. Frankie said we are still waiting on a few people, but they wouldn't be here till tonight." She grabbed the spatula and went back to the stove.

The sliding glass door to the back deck opened, and everyone poured in. Sammy sat beside me, but not before she rolled her eyes at Rachel. I raised my eyebrows at her. Did she really do that?

"I see you met my girl. Wait till you taste her cooking." Frankie kissed Rachel on the cheek.

"I made an egg bake with a hollandaise sauce." Rachel pulled the Pyrex out of the oven.

Frankie helped her dish out everyone's plates and poured the sauce over the eggs. It smelled delicious. I had no doubt she really was a fantastic cook. When we were at the store, I wondered why Frankie was so specific about getting certain foods. She must have sent him a list of things she wanted.

Sammy grabbed the plates from Frankie and handed them out. Rex dove into his, gobbling it up before anyone else got theirs. As a football player, I assumed he ate twice the amount of food as an average person.

Matty took his and took a mouthful as Sammy set a plate

in front of me. I stabbed at it with my fork and brought it to my mouth. Matty dropped his plate, and it crashed to the ground.

What the?

He slapped my fork out of my hand. It hit the counter, spilling sauce all over. "Excuse me?" I stammered.

"Carrots!" Matty yelled. "Fucking carrots!"

"Oh, my goodness. I didn't know Matty was allergic to carrots." Rachel grabbed her chest.

"I'm not. Mal is. Like deathly allergic, and the knuckle-head never carries her Epi." Matty's jaw twitched.

"Chill, I brought it this weekend. But I don't understand. We did the shopping. We didn't get carrots." I chewed my lip.

"Nice job, Rachel. Trying to kill my best friend." Sammy tossed a protective arm around me.

"I'm so sorry." Rachel cried. "It'll never happen again. I really am sorry." Rachel turned and ran from the room.

"Really, Sammy?" Frankie snapped at her and then followed Rachel.

I sat there in silence, staring at the plate. I had lied to everyone, as Matty predicted. I had forgotten my Epi. Everyone knows I'm allergic and we were doing the shopping so I didn't think it was a big deal. Besides, it wasn't deathly like Matty said. Only if I don't get to a hospital in time.

"Dude, how did you even taste the carrots?" Rex asked as he was on his second helping.

"I taste my food instead of inhaling it." Matty grabbed some paper towels and started cleaning up.

Jake fixed me a bowl of cereal as the guys cleaned up. Sammy just kept glancing out the sliding glass door toward where Rachel and Frankie were. Sadness crept over her face.

"What's wrong?" I asked.

"I shouldn't have said that. She was trying to be nice and

cook for us, and I snapped. I'm gonna go apologize." She went outside to where Frankie and Rachel were.

Being left alone with the three guys took all the air out of the room. Instead of thinking of anything to say, I ate my cereal with my head down.

"Hey, why does it look like someone died in here?" Billy asked as he entered the kitchen.

"Cause Mal almost did. It was a carrot mistake." Jake half-laughed.

"Well, glad you are still kicking." He pulled me into a hug. I couldn't even wrap my hands around him.

"Since the party is officially here, and I mean me, let's do this." He pulled two beer cans from his pocket, cracked them open, and downed them. I watched in shock as Billy downed two beers in a matter of seconds. He belched loudly and handed me a can.

"Thanks, but I'm good," I said, pushing the can away.

"Suit yourself." He shrugged and popped open another can. "So, what's the plan for the day?"

"I thought we could go out on the boat," Frankie said, walking back into the room with Rachel at his side. "I rented one for the weekend."

"That sounds like a great idea." Jake clapped his hands together.

"Count me in," Rex said, finishing up his plate.

"I'll pass," I said, knowing that boats always nauseated me.

"Suit yourself," Billy said, taking another swig of his beer.

"Oh no, you are coming. I brought Dramamine." Sammy smiled as she entered the kitchen, the tension from her face now gone.

"Ugh, fine, but I'm bringing a book." I scooted off the stool.

We spent the day out on the lake, soaking up the sun and drinking beer. Rachel turned out to be a great cook, and she made us delicious sandwiches for lunch. She made sure to inform me all the carrots had been tossed.

As the day went on, everyone grew more and more relaxed. The guys started telling stories and cracking jokes, and Rachel and Sammy were chatting like old friends. I was still a little uneasy but glad everyone else was having a good time.

CHAPTER 11

Mal

By the time I got off the boat, I could barely stand. I wobbled as I walked back to the house. Swimming in the water was so different from being on a boat rocking around. As I stumbled back to the house, I realized I was drunk. The combination of the sun, the beer, and the motion sickness had taken its toll on me. My stomach turned, and my head spun.

"Hey, you okay?" Sammy walked beside me.

"I think I'm gonna puke." I grabbed her arm for support.

She led me to the bathroom, where I promptly threw up in the toilet. Her hand was on my back, rubbing soothing circles as I retched.

"That's it, let it all out," she murmured.

After a few minutes, I was done. I flushed the toilet and leaned my head against the cool porcelain. I felt awful, but at least the nausea was gone.

"You feeling better?" Sammy asked, handing me a glass of water.

"Yeah, thanks," I said, taking a sip.

"Good. You scared me for a minute there." She sat back on her heels.

"I didn't think I drank that much." I wiped my mouth with toilet paper.

The door opened, and I prayed it wasn't one of the guys. They had already seen me get sick enough for one lifetime. Luckily, it was Rachel. She held out a candy to me. "It's ginger. It should help."

"Thanks," I chewed on the candy. It tasted gross, but the turning in my stomach calmed.

"I gotta, uh, grab something. I'll be back." Sammy stood up and left.

The doorbell rang downstairs, indicating Harry and Donnie were probably here. "Come on, let's go down and join everyone," Rachel said, offering her hand to help me up.

I took it gratefully, still a little shaky. I quickly brushed my teeth before Rachel guided me downstairs. Together, we went to the living room, where the guys were hanging out with Harry and Donnie. Everyone turned to look at us as we entered.

"Feeling better?" Matty asked, concern etched on his face.

"Yeah, thanks to Sammy and Rachel," I replied, smiling weakly.

"Good, because the rest of the party has arrived!" Harry shouted, raising his hands in the air. He was short and had his hair perfectly coiffed. The man had style.

His boyfriend Donnie had on sweatpants and a t-shirt with stains on it. They were the exact opposite, and yet they made the perfect fit.

Behind them were two girls I didn't recognize. One was tiny and had big hair that cascaded down her back. She reminded me of Tinkerbell. The other girl was much taller and had short braids that framed her face's sharp, beautiful features.

"This is Gabby." Harry pointed to Tinkerbell, and then he pointed to Sharp Beauty. "This is Larisa."

"Nice to meet you," I said, trying to sound more enthusiastic than I felt.

"Likewise," Gabby chirped.

Larisa just nodded at me, her expression calm and aloof.

Harry and Donnie made themselves comfortable on the couch while Gabby and Larisa sat in armchairs. The guys grabbed more beers and started chatting with Harry and Donnie. I sat down on the edge of the couch, still a little dizzy.

"Come on, Mal, loosen up," Billy said, slapping me on the back.

"I'm trying," I said, but it was hard. I was shaky and queasy.

Gabby and Larisa seemed content to just sit and watch the guys talk. They didn't say much, but occasionally, one of them would laugh at something someone said.

"I got an idea." Rex jumped up from his spot on the floor. "I saw a fire pit out back."

Everyone jumped up excitedly, ready to have a bonfire. The guys started gathering wood while Harry and Donnie pulled out chairs to sit on. Gabby and Larisa stayed behind, chatting quietly between themselves.

I helped the guys, trying to shake off the lingering dizziness. As I picked up a hefty log, my grip slipped, and it fell towards my foot.

"Watch out!" Rex shouted, grabbing the log before it hit me.

"Thanks." I averted my eyes.

"It's all good. You okay?" He gave me a concerned look.

"Yeah, just a little clumsy," I said, trying to brush it off.

We walked back to the firepit. The guys started building the fire while Harry and Donnie passed out snacks. I sat down next to Sammy, a little more at ease now that the alcohol was working its way out of my system.

The group laughed and cracked open more beers as the fire blazed higher. At some point, Matty pulled out a guitar and handed it to Jake.

Jake began strumming a few chords, and soon, the entire group was singing along to the country songs he played. Even Gabby and Larisa seemed to be enjoying themselves, swaying along to the music. As Jake played, he would catch my gaze and wink at me. I didn't even know he could play, and not only could he play, he was fantastic.

After a while, Jake put down the guitar, even after we all begged him to continue. In all honesty, I could have listened to him play all night. If only for this moment alone, I was glad I came.

"All right. Let's play a game." Billy clapped his hands together. "Two truths and a lie."

Everyone groaned, but Billy was insistent. "Come on, it'll be fun!"

We all sat in a circle, beers in hand, as Gabby went first, telling us two truths and one lie. We had to guess which one was the lie. "I've lived on four different continents. I have a dragon tattoo, and I've never been in love," she said, her voice low and steady.

The group looked at each other, guessing which statement was false.

"I'm gonna say the tattoo." Sammy scratched her chin.

"Nope." She lifted the sleeve of her shirt, revealing a dragon tattoo wrapped around her shoulder.

"Okay, I'm gonna say never been in love," I chimed in.

"Correct!" Gabby grinned, looking pleased with herself.

Next up was Larisa. "I've skydived. I can speak three languages fluently, and I'm a vegetarian," she said, calm and collected.

We all took turns guessing which statement was false, but no one could seem to figure it out. Finally, she revealed the lie. "I've skydived. I'm actually terrified of heights."

Soon, it was my turn. I tried to think of something interesting. Most of my life was boring. "Okay, I've read over a hundred books this year. I'm a virgin." I tapped my chin. "And I got lost for two days in the woods."

"Hold on." Matty held up his hand. "We all know you got lost in the woods. We were part of the search team."

A silence grew over everyone as they debated on which was the truth. The books, or my virginity.

"It's obvious." Rachel waved her hands around. "She's eighteen, the virgin one." Rachel sat back with a smug look on her face.

"Wrong. It's the books. I've only read sixty-two books this year." I sat back and smiled. Rex, Matty, and Jake all glanced at each other.

"I'll go next," Sammy said. "I've kissed three girls in one night, bungee jumped off a bridge, and broken a bone."

The group huddled together, trying to figure out which statement was the lie. I looked over at Sammy, knowing which one was the lie. Everyone else seemed to be contemplating which one was. Obviously, she seemed like the type of person to do all three.

"I'm going with the bone." Rex said, leaning back against the chair.

"Nope." Sammy grinned. Her eyes sparkled. "I've broken my arm twice."

"I'm going with the bungee jumping," Frankie answered.

"Correct!" Sammy exclaimed, throwing her hands up in the air.

The group laughed and joked around, enjoying each other's company. I was relaxed and having a good time, something that hadn't happened in a while. As the night wore on and the embers died down, people started to head to bed.

At one point, it was only Rex, Matty, Jake, Sammy, and me left. I kept trying to get Sammy's attention so she would get the hint and go upstairs. I couldn't say anything without it being obvious that I wanted her to go.

Finally, Sammy got up and winked at me. I tried to keep my face steady and try not to show the fact that every atom of my being was excited to be left alone with them.

CHAPTER 12

Mal

"READY TO FINISH THAT GAME OF TRUTH OR DARE?" Jake winked at me.

My heart raced in my chest. This was it, my chance to potentially hook up with all three. I wasn't talking about sex, just some kissing. Okay, maybe a little more.

"Sure," I mumbled.

Matty went first, choosing dare. Jake grinned mischievously, "I dare you to do a 60-second lap dance for Mal."

I blushed furiously as Matty stood up, swaying his hips to an imaginary beat. I couldn't help but giggle as he shook his butt in my face. When the minute ended, we all clapped and cheered.

Rex went next, choosing truth. I asked him a mundane question, but when it was Jake's turn, he chose dare.

"I dare you to kiss Mal for 30 seconds," he said, his eyes never leaving mine.

My heart raced as Jake leaned in and pressed his lips to mine. It was a soft, sweet kiss, but it still made my head spin. When the timer beeped, I was gasping for air.

"Mal, truth or dare?" Jake asked as I was still panting.

"Dare," I said, trying to sound confident.

"I dare you to make out with all three of us for a minute each," Jake smirked.

My eyes widened as I realized what he was asking. I had never done anything like this before, but I couldn't deny the excitement that was pulsing through me. Without thinking, I leaned in to Jake, my lips meeting his in a fiery embrace.

Rex and Matty moved in as we kissed, their hands caressing my back and thighs. Soon, Jake swapped places with Rex, and he was just as passionate. I could feel their eyes watching me as I surrendered to the moment.

Matty was last, his was the deepest, and he held me tight against him. His desire for me sent a shiver down my spine.

When the minute was up, I pulled away, smiling. I looked around at the circle. Jake got up and tossed a few more logs on the fire, indicating we weren't stopping anytime soon.

"Rex, which one?" I asked.

"Without question, dare." Rex winked at me.

I took a deep breath. How far could I push this? How far was I willing to go?

"Suck on Mal's nipples," Jake spoke up before I had a chance.

"Isn't Mal supposed to dare him?" Matty asked.

"No, I'm fine with that." I slowly pulled my shirt over my head and unclipped my bra.

Rex took a deep breath and looked at me, his eyes burning with need. He leaned in and gently took one of my taut nipples between his teeth, and my breath hitched. He licked and nibbled gently, sending shockwaves through my body. My panties were soaked.

"Damn, okay, Mal, your turn, and please pick dare." Rex licked his lips.

"Okay, dare." The warmth from the fire caressed my nipples. I wanted them so badly.

"Grind on each one of our laps until we are hard." Rex leaned back in his chair.

I smiled. That wasn't too bad. I stood up and walked over to Matty, sitting on his lap and grinding on him. Matty's eyes were wide, and his mouth hung open as I rotated my hips, pressing my pussy against his very hard cock.

"Damn, I'm hard already." Matty swallowed.

I stood and moved to Jake, who I straddled and grinded against, feeling his cock throb against my thigh. I moaned lightly and moved to Rex, who lifted me up and sat me on his lap.

"We are all competing for your attention," Jake said, his voice low and seductive.

"How do I choose?" I grinned as I ground my hips against Rex's cock. My pussy throbbed as I rubbed against him.

"No one is making you. We can all have fun. After all, it is a game." Jake smiled. The flames from the fire glinted in his eyes.

"Jake, your turn." Matty scooted his chair closer.

"Obviously dare." He bit his lip.

"I want you to lick Mal's pussy until she is about to cum and then stop." Matty's voice was low and husky.

Rex shifted quickly and turned me around, so I was sitting on his lap. Matty came over and slid my jeans off. My heart raced. I had never had a guy go down on me before. Jake walked over and kneeled in front of me.

My pussy throbbed. I wanted him to touch me, to feel his hands on me and push me over the edge with his tongue. I leaned back on Rex and spread my legs, exposing my soaked pussy to him. He pulled my panties aside and ran his tongue up and down my slit. I moaned as my body tensed.

Jake started at my entrance and moved up, licking me

slowly. I was so ready to cum, when he slid a finger into my tight hole, I almost exploded. He slowly slid his finger in and out of my dripping pussy. He swirled his tongue around my clit, and I knew I wouldn't last much longer. I was already so close. It was so hot, and I didn't want it to stop.

Jake lowered his mouth and started to slide his tongue inside me. The softness of his tongue thrusting in and out of me was almost enough to push me over the edge. I moaned loudly as he switched and slid his fingers in and out of me. I was so close, so close.

"I'm so close," I moaned loudly.

He gently sucked my clit into his mouth. As he sucked on my swollen bud, my pussy clenched. As I was about to cum he stopped. My pussy throbbed. Fuck, I needed to cum.

"Matty, truth or dare." Jake looked over at him.

"Dare." Matty had a serious look on his face.

"I dare you to go down on Mal until she cums. Do not stop, no matter what." Jake grinned as he got up and sat in his chair.

I looked at him and saw the fire in his eyes. He wanted me to cum on his friend's face, to share me with them. Fuck, was I dreaming?

"Done." Matty came over and knelt in front of me.

I moaned softly as he slid his tongue in and out of me, gently sucking my clit into his mouth. His tongue slid in and out of my entrance, bringing me closer and closer. I moaned loudly as Jake stood up and walked over to me; he put his hand on the back of Matty's head, pushing his face deeper into my pussy.

I moaned loudly as my body tensed. I was so close I could already feel the build-up.

"That's it, Mal, I know you are going to cum," Jake said softly.

"I want to," I moaned.

"You will when Matty lets you," Jake whispered into my ear.

"I can't, I need to. Please," I pleaded.

"You're not going to until Matty tells you to," Jake whispered.

I moaned loudly, the intensity building. Rex reached his hands around me and played with my nipples.

My body was on fire.

"Not yet," Jake whispered.

I was so close. My whole body tensed, my pussy throbbed. I couldn't stop it now. I was about to explode.

"Not until Matty says." His voice was a low whisper as he leaned in and took my earlobe in his mouth.

"I'm about to, please," I begged.

Matty sucked on my clit and pinched my nipple. He was playing my body like an instrument. As he sucked on my clit, the orgasm building.

Rex pinched my nipples and kissed my neck as Matty continued to devour my quivering pussy.

"Damn, Mal, you taste so good. I want to feel you orgasm in my mouth." Matty moaned, his warm breath hitting me.

"Fuck," I whimpered.

Matty's tongue flicked my clit, and I gasped, pushing my pussy against him as my body tensed. Jake pushed Matty's head down again as my orgasm crashed over me. My body tensed. I moaned and gyrated against Matty. My body spasmed as I came harder than I ever had. I had never experienced anything like it. Every inch of me tingled as hundreds of tiny orgasms rocked me.

"Good girl," Jake stood back and unzipped his pants. "Now, suck my cock."

"Yes," I moaned. My body was still throbbing from my orgasm.

I leaned over and slid Jake's pants down, exposing his long, hard cock.

"Fuck baby, your pussy was so sweet." Jake groaned as he slid his hand through my hair and pulled my head back.

I was so wet my juices were dripping down my thighs. I wrapped my lips around his head, running my tongue around his shaft. He tasted salty, and he sighed as I slid down his shaft. He was so big. I didn't think I could fit him all in my mouth. I tried, and he groaned, grabbing the back of my head. I raised up and licked his shaft. I ran my tongue around his head, and he sucked in a breath. I slid down on him again and again. Jake got harder by the second.

"Mal, that is so damn good." He moaned as I took him all the way in.

I slid up and down, and he sucked in a breath. His cock pulsated in my mouth. He gripped my hair and groaned loudly. I moaned and wrapped my hand around the base of his shaft, my mouth sucking on him.

Rex slid his hands from my nipples and down my body. He slid them between my legs and started to rub my clit. I slid Jake's cock from my mouth, barely able to concentrate.

"I want you to cum as I explode in your mouth," Jake whispered, pulling my head back.

Rex slid his finger inside me. I was so wet and so close. Rex rubbed my clit as fast as he could, and the warmth growing inside me. I gasped as he pushed a second finger into my pussy.

I was throbbing and pulsing, my body ready to explode. I took Jake back into my mouth as Rex's finger fucked me. The heat burned inside me. I moaned louder as he shoved his fingers into my pussy. I sucked on Jake's cock, harder than ever. I was so ready for my orgasm, it was building up as his cock swelled in my mouth.

"I'm about to shoot my load in your mouth," Jake growled.

I mumbled around his cock, and the first wave of my orgasm crashed over me. As it washed over me, I thrust my pussy up as Rex pressed his fingers into me. Jake's cock swelled in my mouth, and I came harder. My body was spasming as wave after wave crashed over me.

"You are such a good girl," Jake moaned.

His cock pulsed, and I swallowed him. He grunted loudly as he exploded in my mouth. His warm cum slid down my throat. I took all of him, sucking him dry.

Rex wrapped his arms around me as I leaned into him. My body was on fire. This was my dream. I wanted to pinch myself to make sure this was really happening.

"Fuck that was so hot. I think we should call it a night." Matty checked his watch. "I'm actually surprised no one came out here with all the noise we were making."

"What about you two?" I pointed to Rex and Matty.

"There is always tomorrow. We don't wanna wear you out before this has even begun." Rex kissed the top of my head.

CHAPTER 13

Mal

SAMMY WAS ON MY BED CUDDLING MY PILLOW WHEN I got out of the shower. She had a sly smile on her face and stared at me as I walked over to my bag. As I got dressed, I could feel her eyes on me.

"Are you gonna tell me what happened or are you gonna make me beg?" Sammy huffed.

"I spent last night with Jake, Rex, and Matty," I giggled.

"I knew it, I fucking knew it. I can't believe you. Did you have fun?" She laughed.

"You have no idea." I blushed.

"Well, tell me all about it," Sammy pouted.

I flopped on the bed next to her. I was getting warm. Just talking about it made me want to do it all over again. I told her everything that had happened, and she listened intently and smiled the whole time. It was so good to have someone to talk to about this. I could tell her anything and she would never judge me. I was so lucky to have her.

"So, what do you think? Is it weird that I like three guys at once?" I asked.

"Nah, it's cool. Just wish I could find three guys that hot to fool around with me at the same time." She slapped my arm.

"Ha, maybe someday you will. What are we doing today?" I asked.

"Well, it's almost noon. So almost everyone is gone. No one wanted to bother you." Sammy chewed her lip.

"Gone?"

"Yeah, Frankie, Rachel, Donnie, Harry, and Larisa went for another boat ride. Since your whole seasick thing, they didn't bother waking you to see if you wanted to go."

"And everyone else?" I asked.

"Gabby and Billy went for a swim and your men are fishing." Sammy smiled, but I knew it was fake.

"Oh no, I'm sorry. I know you were into Billy." I pulled her in for a hug.

"It's fine. I have too many men to keep track of, anyway." She swatted me away.

"So, what are we gonna do?" I asked, changing the subject.

"We have options. We could go swimming, or fishing, or watch a movie." Sammy tapped her chin. "I'm even down to reading all day."

Sammy loved books like I did. Maybe not as much, but she could devour a dark romance book in a day.

"Why don't we lay out by the water and read?" I shrugged. "That way we can also get some vitamin D. Best of both worlds."

"That's a damn good idea." She smiled. "I'll get my book and we can throw a blanket out. You want something to drink?"

"Yeah, that sounds good." I walked over to my bag and pulled out the sexy one-piece I had bought.

Since I was on the beach, I figured it was the perfect time to wear something so revealing. I looked at myself in the mirror and smiled. I did look pretty hot. The top was strapless, and the bottoms were high-cut. I slipped it on, and it hugged my curves perfectly.

"So, what do you think?" I turned around and twirled.

"You look fucking hot. And those boys are going to be in a frenzy." Sammy laughed.

My cheeks turned red. I didn't know how to reply to compliments. To try to not sound silly, I nodded and grabbed my book, then followed her outside.

We laid out on the blankets and cracked open our books. Mine was the latest Melody Caraballo book. The girl knew how to write a compelling story. I flipped through the pages and tried to concentrate.

I glanced over to the group of guys. They were all off in their own little fishing spots. I watched as they cast their lines and then turned away. I was trying to concentrate. The words weren't even making sense to me. I heard footsteps in the grass, and I looked up to see Rex slowly walking towards me.

I grinned up at him. He was wearing a pair of shorts and nothing else. His muscular chest and abs were on full display, towering over me.

"Hey, beautiful." He grinned. "How are you doing?"

"Pretty good," I smiled.

He got closer, and the citrus in his cologne was intoxicating. He sat next to me, blocking my view of Sammy. His hand grazed my thigh, sending a chill up my spine.

My heart pounded in my chest as his fingers traced up and down my thigh. I was already wet.

"How's fishing going?" I asked, trying to ignore the way his touch set my body on fire.

"Not bad, wanna do some fishing with me?" he asked.

"Sure, why not," I said.

"Count me out." Sammy didn't lift her head from her book.

"Change your mind and we will be down there." Rex

pointed toward the edge of the lake. His eyes sparkled, and I wanted to jump on him. He stood and reached his hand out for me. I took it and followed him to the end of the lake.

My heart was racing as he handed me a pole. I tried to act normal, but I was so excited to be around him.

"I don't do very well with fish," I laughed. My hands trembled when I gripped the pole.

"Aw, you'll do great." He chuckled. "Just try your best."

"Probably not." I stared at the pole. What the heck was I supposed to do?

"I'll show you." He stepped behind me and wrapped his arms around my waist. His hands rested on top of mine. "Like this." He showed me how to cast the line. "If you hook anything, you pull it in. Okay?"

"But what if catch a fish?" I asked.

"Then you pull it in." He smirked.

We stood there next to each other for a few minutes. I tried to concentrate on fishing, but his arms around me made it impossible to think. He kissed my temple, and I let out a deep breath. I wanted him so badly.

"I wish I could bend you over in this bathing suit right now," he whispered in my ear.

Every hair on me stood up as electricity pulsed through my body. I pressed my legs together, trying to concentrate on the fishing.

The pole tugged in my hands. "Oh my! I think I have one!" I yelped as I pulled whatever was on the other end of the line. As it got closer to shore, I could see that it was huge. "Holy cow, Rex! It's a monster!"

"It's a bass. Reel it in." Rex's hands covered mine as we reeled it in.

Together we fought with the fish. The thing kept struggling to stay in the water. My arms ached as I tried to reel it up. I held on to the pole as hard as I could and looked back at Rex, who was trying to help me. Together, we reeled it in until it didn't struggle anymore. I held my breath as I looked at the bass.

"Holy shit." I laughed as it flopped around.

"We got him." Rex grinned and picked up the fish. He dropped it in the nearest bucket and winked at me.

"Nice job." Jake walked over to us and high-fived me.

"You should always be in a bathing suit. Such a nice view." Matty also joined us.

Blush rose to my cheeks as the guys surrounded me, admiring the bass and my one-piece swimsuit.

"Alright, let's get this cleaned up." Rex grabbed the bucket and started to head back to the house.

"I'll help you." I followed him.

"So will we." Jake lifted me up and tossed me over his shoulder. "Ya know, no one is at the house right now."

We entered the house, and Jake set me down on the counter. Rex set the bucket down and practically pushed Jake out of the way. His lips were on mine, sending sparks through my body as he kissed me.

My hands found their way to the back of his head as I pulled him closer to me. I wanted him, and I wanted him now. Rex's hands roamed down my body and landed on my hips, pulling me closer to him. I could feel his hardness through his shorts, and it only made me want him more.

"Fuck, you're so beautiful," he muttered against my lips.

"I want you," I breathed out, and he chuckled.

"Patience, baby. We'll get there," he said, trailing kisses down my neck.

My fingers tangled in his hair as he found my sweet spot. I moaned, and he smirked against my skin.

"You like that?" he asked, and I could only nod.

He slid my bathing suit to the side and dove in. Rex's tongue slid up and down my clit already sending me on edge. I leaned back and watched Jake's and Matty's reactions. Both of them bit their lips with desire in their eyes.

I was so close.

Rex pulled back from my pussy and looked up at me. "I didn't get my chance last night."

"I'm glad you are now," I moaned.

"Guys, hurry up. Sammy is coming." Matty stood taller, trying to block the view.

Sammy walked in barely looking into the kitchen. Matty and Jake stood in front of us. She flopped into the dining room chair.

"Did you two see Mal?" Sammy asked. "I brought her book in. I needed a break from the sun."

"Nope," Jake mumbled.

I was so close. Rex devoured my pussy.

Matty coughed loudly. "No."

Rex reached up and covered my mouth. I ground my teeth as I reached the edge. As I orgasmed Matty continued to cough.

"Weird. I thought she came in here with Rex. Oh, maybe they are, ya know, upstairs," Sammy giggled.

"Maybe. You should go check," Jake said. "It would be funny."

"No, she deserves to get her world rocked. I'm gonna go lay down. If you see her, could you tell her that her book is here?" Sammy replied.

As soon as she left, Rex removed his hand. Matty and Jake let out sighs and I slumped down. Holy cow, that was close. We all busted out laughing at the same time.

"What's so funny?" Frankie stepped into the room with the rest of the group.

"Uh, nothing." Jake grabbed the bucket and set it on the counter. "We are preparing dinner."

CHAPTER 14

Mal

FRANKIE HAD TO HAVE KNOWN SOMETHING WAS UP. He refused to leave us alone. He even gutted some of the fish, horribly, but he still did it. He was so protective, I hated it.

Before dinner, we had a bonfire. The guys gathered some wood, and Frankie started the fire. It was chilly by the lake, but all I could think about was the night before.

"Should we get blankets?" Sammy asked. "I'm freezing."

"Yes please." Gabby rubbed her arms.

"I have some in the house," Frankie said as he stood.

"I can go get them," I offered.

"No, it's okay," Sammy and Frankie said at the same time.

"Sammy." Frankie turned to her. "You look after the fire, I'll go get them."

He walked off, and I looked at Sammy. She picked at her nails and stared at the fire. Frankie and Sammy usually got along really well. This weekend it was almost as if he was avoiding her. It didn't make sense.

Matty got up and started the grill. Rachel got up to help but he told her he had this meal. As long as I had known Matty, he had been cooking. His parents once said if he didn't do well as a teacher he could always fall back on cooking. Not that they would be happy with that, but it was better than not having a plan B.

Frankie showed back up and handed out blankets to everyone that was cold. When Sammy took one they didn't even look at each other. Very odd.

"So what are we doing tomorrow?" I asked. Maybe I would set my alarm and actually wake up at a reasonable time.

"Harry and I have to leave early." Donnie kissed Harry's hand.

"Yeah us too." Gabby nodded toward Larisa.

"Same here." Billy winked at Gabby.

"Don't worry, we will say goodbye tonight. We know you sleep in." Harry smiled.

"What can I say, I like sleep." I shrugged.

"So what are we gonna do tomorrow?" Rachel asked.

"There is a hiking trail on the north end of the lake. We could all go." Rex tossed another log on the fire.

We all agreed to go on the hike the next day, so I had to bite the bullet and actually wake up at a decent time. When it was time to call it a night, everyone said their goodbyes and went to their separate rooms.

Sammy came into our room and sat on my bed. I grabbed my stuff for a shower but kept glancing at Sammy, but she seemed quieter than usual. I was about to ask her if everything was okay when she spoke up.

"Can I tell you something?" She asked, her voice dripping with apprehension.

"Of course," I said reflexively. Sammy had never been nervous about talking, so this must have been serious.

She took a deep breath. "Frankie and I...were kinda together." She finally said after what felt like an eternity of silence.

I couldn't believe my ears. Frankie and Sammy? It didn't make sense; he was my brother and she was my best friend!

But then again, maybe this was why he had been avoiding her all weekend? Either way, it was clear that there were some feelings between them and he now had a girlfriend. Neither one of them would cheat, there was no way they would.

I nodded slowly as I tried to process this information. "When...um when did this happen?" I finally asked hesitantly. It was wrong to pry into her business like this but at the same time, if Frankie cheated, I would have a big problem with that.

Sammy looked up shaking her head. "It was a few months ago," she whispered. "Before he got with Rachel."

I let out a deep breath. "Good."

"I would never touch someone that was with someone." She picked at the comforter. "I'm jealous and trying so hard not to be. It wasn't serious and it was before Rachel, so why does my heart clamp up when I see him? I mean, we were talking for a while. I thought we had something."

"Ugh, I can't even be mad at you for being with my brother when you look all sad." I joined her on the bed and put my arm around her. "Look, this whole thing will blow over."

At least that explained why Frankie was avoiding her. He either had feelings for her or he didn't want to be around someone he had been with in the past. Since Frankie was super loyal when it came to girls, it was probably the latter.

"Thanks. I'm gonna get some sleep." Sammy hugged me, then got up and crawled into her bed.

Somehow I had managed to fall asleep rather quickly. Of course that didn't mean I wanted to get up early. Mornings were meant for birds, not me.

I rolled over and turned off my alarm. I was sure Frankie was up and ready to go, so I should have been in a rush to get up. My stomach was a little unsettled, so I told myself I would just lay in bed for a bit.

"Mal," Sammy spoke sharply. "Are you getting up? It's nearly seven."

I groaned, "I just want to lie here."

"You have to get up. We are going on a hike, remember?" Sammy yanked the covers.

I sat up and looked at her. "How could I forget?"

The door creaked open and Matty poked his head in. "Did you manage to wake the princess?"

"I'm working on it," Sammy sighed.

I grabbed my pillow and tossed it at Matty, he slammed the door before the pillow hit him. He whistled as he walked away.

"I'm up!" I yelled and stood.

I quickly brushed my hair and teeth and put on a little bit of makeup. I slipped on some leggings and a cute T-shirt and walked into the living room.

"Hey guys," I said as I plopped on the sofa next to Rex.

"Mal, I'm glad you're awake." Rex kissed me on the cheek. "We have to go soon. I think everyone else is almost ready."

"I just have to get my shoes," I said as I stood. I walked across the room to the front door.

I was just about to slip on my shoes when I heard Frankie come in. "How could you do that to me?" Frankie's voice was thick with hurt.

"Frankie, I-."

Shit, this was it. He found out about me hooking up with his best friends. Someone had to have seen us by the fire or in the kitchen. Maybe he saw Rex kiss my cheek. I didn't know how, but somehow he found out.

My heart pounded in my chest as I turned to look at him. His hand was over his heart and his eyes were staring into my soul.

"The two of you should be ashamed." He pointed at me then Rex.

"I can explain." Rex stood and put his hands up.

"You should know better." Frankie glared at Rex.

"Excuse me, I'm an adult. I can make my own decisions." I placed my hand on my hip. I got that he was upset but he didn't get to blame all of this on Rex.

"Oh please. I'm shocked you are up this early. I can't expect you to also feed yourself." Frankie crossed his arms.

"Huh?" Rex and I asked simultaneously.

"Breakfast." Frankie shook his head. "You two can't expect to go on a hike without eating. Rex, you're an athlete, you know better." Frankie turned and walked back into the kitchen.

I let out a sigh of relief, glad that Frankie wasn't upset about anything else. But my stomach churned with guilt. I knew that what had happened between his friends and I wasn't right, but I couldn't help myself. Frankie had no idea that his best friends had been hooking up with his sister, and I wasn't about to tell him.

I walked into the kitchen and saw that Matty, Sammy, and Jake were already there, eating pancakes that Rachel had made.

"Morning, everyone," I said, trying to sound cheerful.

"Good morning, Mal," Rachel said with a smile. "I made pancakes for everyone. Help yourself."

"Thanks, Rach." I grabbed a plate and started piling pancakes on it.

"Are you excited for the hike?" Jake asked me.

"Yeah, it should be fun," I said, trying to act like everything was normal. "As long as I don't fall or break something."

Frankie walked over to me and put his arm around my shoulders. "You're going to do fine."

I smiled up at him, still tense from thinking he had caught

us. I made a mental note to talk to the guys later and figure out how to handle the situation.

We finished breakfast quickly and headed out to the trail-head. It was a beautiful day, the sun was shining and there was a light breeze that kept us cool. We chatted and joked as we walked along the trail, enjoying the fresh air and the beautiful scenery.

Sammy walked beside me, and I could tell that she was still bothered by what she had told me last night. I tried to cheer her up by making silly jokes and telling her funny stories, but she just smiled weakly and seemed lost in thought.

As we hiked higher up the mountain, the terrain became more challenging, and we had to scramble over rocks and steep inclines. My heart pounded in my chest, and my legs were burning. This was not exactly my idea of a fun day, but I got to hang out with my friends. As an added bonus, watching Jake, Matty, and Rex walk ahead of me was a treat all on its own.

"Are you okay?" I tossed my arm around Sammy.

"Yeah, I'm just having a little trouble," Sammy sighed.

"Same." I trudged up the trail.

"Oh, not the hike," Sammy laughed. "No, I mean Frankie and Rachel. It would be so much easier if Rachel wasn't the nicest girl ever. You know she felt so bad about the carrots in the weird egg dish she made, she cried."

"I didn't know that. She is really nice." I took in a deep breath. "How is this hike not killing you?"

"Aside from all the sexual exercise I get, I run every morning." Sammy jogged a little ahead of me then turned and jogged backward.

"Now you are just showing off."

"A little. Come on, do a little jog with me." Sammy continued to run backward.

Everyone else was way ahead of us. I couldn't be hurt that

97

the guys were so far ahead, we couldn't let on that there was anything between us. Frankie would get suspicious if they hung around Sammy and me.

"Come on," Sammy taunted again.

I rolled my eyes, but then I started to run with her, laughing as we raced each other up the trail. We ran together for a few moments, our laughter echoing through the trees.

The burn of actually exercising ran through my body. Everything ached. There was no reason for people to actually run, it wasn't fun.

"You are doing good." Sammy slapped my back and then ran faster. "Catch me or I'll tell all your secrets."

"Not funny." I chased after her.

She giggled as she taunted me. I pushed hard as I ran. My body was ready to give up. It was too early, I was too tired, I was too out-of-shape, I was not a runner.

My foot caught. I fell forward. I braced for the fall and still managed to slam into the ground. Pain shot up my leg as I landed. I winced, realizing that I had twisted my ankle. I tried to get up, but the pain was too much.

"Mal, are you okay?" I heard Rex calling out to me.

"I'm fine," I yelled back, even though I was anything but. "Just twisted my ankle a little."

Rex and the others ran back towards me, the worry etched on their faces.

"It's okay," I said, trying to sound casual. "I just need to rest a little. You guys go on ahead, I'll catch up."

"No way," Frankie said, shaking his head. "We're not leaving you here by yourself."

Matty and Sammy sat down on the ground beside me, while the others stood around, looking concerned.

"I'll carry you." Jake winked at me.

CHAPTER 15

Mal

I REFUSED MULTIPLE TIMES FOR ANYONE TO CARRY me. I could take care of myself, even if that meant hobbling down the rest of the hiking trail. The problem was that everyone wanted to go up the rest of the trail to see the view. I didn't want to be the person to put a damper on things and request we all head back to the lake house. So, I finally allowed Jake to carry me.

I tried to hide the blush on my cheeks as he hoisted me up onto his back. I wrapped my arms around his neck and held on tight, feeling his muscles ripple beneath my fingers. It was kind of nice to be carried that way.

"Ready?" Jake asked, his voice low and rumbling.

I nodded, my heart pounding in my chest. Jake started walking, his long legs eating up the distance effortlessly. I wanted to keep my arms around him forever. But I knew that it wasn't possible. Jake was one of Frankie's best friends, and I didn't want to complicate things between us. I tried to push those thoughts aside and enjoy the ride.

We made our way up the mountain, him carrying me as if I weighed nothing. The others followed behind us, chatting and laughing as if nothing had happened. Jake's muscles tensed and relaxed beneath me as he walked, his breaths coming in slow and steady.

As we reached the top, an incredible view of the valley greeted us below. The mountains rose around us, their peaks shrouded in mist. Birds dove in and out of view, adding to the majestic landscape.

"It's beautiful," I whispered, my voice catching in my throat.

Jake lowered me to the ground, and I stepped away from him. I was a little self-conscious about how much I had enjoyed being carried. But when I looked up at him, I saw a glint in his eyes that told me he had enjoyed it just as much as I had.

We all sat down on a flat rock as Rachel opened her bookbag and started handing out drinks to everyone. Sammy averted her eyes as she took one. Had I not known how she felt about Frankie, I probably wouldn't have even noticed.

Frankie kissed the top of Rachel's head as he took his, then turned to look at everyone. He scratched his chin and kept messing with the cap of the water bottle.

"Guys, I appreciate you all coming out to the lake house and spending the weekend with me. Today is the hardest day of the year." He looked down as if studying a patch of dirt. "I love you all and am glad you guys are my family. Rest in peace, Mom." Frankie poured some water on the ground.

When our mom was going through chemo, she was severely dehydrated. One of the many awful side effects of the medicine. As a joke, she would always tell us to drink more for her, as if that would help her. Yet, we always did. Anytime we drank water we would cheer and say 'Here's to you, Mom.' After she passed away, we kept doing it. Now on her anniversary, we pour some out for her.

Tears stung my eyes as Frankie spoke, his voice choking

with emotion. This day meant so much to us and we were lucky to spend it with our friends. We all raised our water bottles and repeated the familiar words, "Here's to you, Mom."

After a few moments of silence, we all settled in and enjoyed the scenery. We chatted and joked, taking in the peacefulness of nature.

As the sun rose high in the sky, we started to make our way back down the trail. I was still limping, but the pain had subsided somewhat. Jake walked beside me, his hand on my elbow, ready to help me if I stumbled.

"Thanks for carrying me," I said, looking up at him.

"Anytime," he replied with a grin.

"Hey any of us would have loved to carry you," Matty said as he slapped Jake's back.

"Hey, calm down, that's my sister." Frankie wagged his finger at Matty.

"Relax, Frankie." Rex shook Frankie's shoulders. "He was kidding."

Desperate to change the subject, I said the first thing that entered my mind. "Don't you think it's weird dad hasn't even called?"

The group fell silent at my question, and I instantly regretted bringing it up. My dad had been distant since my mom's death, and it had only gotten worse in recent months. I knew he had his way of dealing with things, but it still hurt that he wasn't there for us like he used to be.

"I'm sure he's just busy," Sammy offered, but even she didn't sound convinced.

"Yeah, probably swamped with work," Rex added, but his tone was tinged with doubt.

I sighed, knowing that they were just trying to make me feel better. But the truth was, I was worried about my dad. I missed him, and I didn't know how to bridge the gap between us.

We continued in silence, lost in our thoughts. As we made our way back to the lake house, I couldn't stop the turning in my stomach. Something was off, and I didn't know what it was.

When we finally arrived, everyone scattered to do their own thing. Rachel went to the kitchen to start making dinner, while Frankie joined her to help. Matty went down to the dock to fish, Sammy went to our room to read, and Rex disappeared into the guest room.

Jake lingered behind, looking at me with concern in his eyes. "You okay?" he asked, his hand hovering over my shoulder.

I nodded, but he didn't seem convinced. "Is it your ankle?" he asked.

"No, it's not that. My ankle is doing much better," I replied, swallowing hard. "It's just...I don't know. Something feels off today."

Jake nodded, understanding in his eyes. "I get that," he said. "Today is a tough day for you. You're allowed to feel off."

I smiled at him, grateful for his understanding. "Thanks," I mumbled.

Jake leaned in and brushed his lips against mine. It was a gentle kiss, full of tenderness and affection.

I pulled back, terrified that at any moment Frankie would walk in and see. He would flip if he found out I was hooking up with his best friend. He would kill me if he knew it was all three of them.

"I think I'm gonna call my dad." I bit my lip and pulled out my phone.

"Would you like privacy or company?" Jake took my hand and kissed it.

"Company, thank you." I clicked on my dad's contact.

After a few rings, he finally answered. "Hey, what's up?" There was laughter in his voice mixed with heavy breathing.

"What's up? You know what today is." I ground my teeth. How did he sound so carefree?

"Oh, yeah. I know, honey," he sighed. All his laughter was gone.

"Honey? Who are you on the phone with?" A woman's voice asked in the background.

I hung up.

How could he? How dare he? I tried to concentrate on my breathing.

Jake wrapped his arms around me, sensing my distress. "What happened?" he asked softly.

I shook my head, tears streaming down my face. "He was with someone else," I whispered, feeling the weight of my dad's betrayal crushing me.

Jake held me tighter, his hand rubbing soothing circles on my back. "I'm so sorry," he murmured, his voice full of sympathy.

Backing away from him, I wiped my tears with my hand. "I can't do this," my voice shook with anger and hurt. "I can't deal with my dad. He was with another woman and didn't bother to tell us."

Jake looked at me, his eyes full of understanding. "Then don't," he said simply.

"What do you mean?" I scrunched up my face.

"I mean, don't deal. Or do and talk to me or Frankie."

My phone rang. My father was calling me back. I sent it to voicemail. He called two more times before I shut off my phone.

"I choose to not deal." I clicked on the TV and tried to watch Gordon Ramsey.

"Fine by me." Jake leaned back and pulled on the recliner.

Two minutes later, Frankie came barging into the room

with his phone in his hand. "You called Dad, hung up on him, and then don't take his calls? What is wrong with you, Mal?"

"Did he even tell you why?" I yelled.

"Yeah, he said you overreacted." Frankie shook his head. "Said you were probably upset that he isn't here. That's still no reason to hang up on him!"

"Overreacted? Ha." I crossed my arms and turned back to the TV. I'll show him overreacting.

"Dude, she has a reason to be upset." Jake stood and walked toward the kitchen. "Talk to her instead of yelling at her."

Frankie's face fell, realization dawning on him. "What happened?" he asked, his voice softening.

"He was with another woman," I said, my voice breaking with emotion. "I called him, and he was with her. He didn't even bother to tell us he had moved on."

Frankie's eyes widened, his expression one of shock and disbelief. "I can't believe him," he muttered, his fists clenched. "He told me he wasn't going to tell you. Not like this."

"You knew? You knew, and you didn't say anything?" I stood and stormed into the kitchen, ignoring the slight tinge of pain in my ankle. As I passed him, I growled, "fuck you."

CHAPTER 16

Rex

I CHASED AFTER MAL. WATCHING HER IN SO MUCH pain destroyed me. I knew Mal since we were kids and I always hated seeing her cry. It was like seeing an angel fall.

Not that she cried much as a kid. Even though she was extremely clumsy, she always managed to hide her pain. The girl was strong. Maybe that was why my heart beat only for her. Everyone assumed I stayed single because I was so focused on football. That wasn't true. It was her. It was always her.

I found Mal sitting on the wooden dock, her feet dangling over the edge. I hesitated for a moment before sitting down next to her. She didn't look at me, but I could tell she was still crying.

"I'm sorry," I breathed. "I didn't know."

Mal finally looked at me, her eyes red and puffy. "It's not your fault," she said, her voice hoarse. "I just...I can't believe he would do this."

I wrapped my arm around her, pulling her close to my chest. "I'm here for you," I whispered, my lips brushing against her temple.

Mal leaned into me, her head resting on my shoulder. "Thank you," she murmured, her words barely audible.

We sat there in silence for a while, the sound of the water lapping against the shore was the only noise. I didn't know what to say, so I just held her, hoping that my presence was enough.

After a while, she pulled back and looked into my eyes. "How could he move on?"

I shrugged. "My whole life I have only had eyes for one girl. I don't know how someone could have feelings for another person."

Her face flushed red as she looked at the lake, avoiding my words. She had to know I was talking about her.

"Remember when we were kids and Frankie would make me cry?" She swung her feet and picked at her nails. "You would chase after me then too and make me laugh."

One night in particular never left my mind. There was a high school dance Mal wanted to go to. She had talked about it for weeks. It was her first official dance.

She dyed blue strands in her hair to match her dress. Her parents had given her permission to go on the stipulation that Frankie went. As a senior, he had outgrown silly dances, or so he said.

Mal begged Frankie to go. She tried bribing him with money, to do his chores for a month, to wash his car, anything. He would have gone had Matty, Jake, and I not bought him Coldplay tickets.

I was there when she was screaming at Frankie for not going to the dance. She begged him one last time to go. He yelled at her, refusing to go. When she ran out of the house, I chased after her.

"Mal, stop." I ran down the street.

"Please, Rex." She turned and wiped at her tears. "This is embarrassing enough without you."

I wanted to make her pain disappear. We should have never gotten those tickets. In truth, it was my idea. I was jealous and didn't want her to go to the dance. Not when I couldn't be the one to take her. Frankie had already warned us all that his sister was off-limits. So my stupid, jealous plan was to prevent her from dating anyone.

"You have nothing to be embarrassed about when it comes to me." I grabbed her and pulled her into me.

"Really? I'm sobbing over not going to a dance." She wrapped her arms around me.

That was the moment I knew it was only her. She had my heart. I lifted her chin to look into her eyes. I didn't care what her brother said. Mal was mine. I leaned down to reach her lips.

"Fine!" Frankie shouted from behind us.

We both jumped and separated.

"I hate when you cry, Mal." He joined us and glared at me. Probably for hugging his little sister. "The guys can get someone else to go with them to the concert. I'll go with you to homecoming."

We never did go to the concert. We sold our tickets and went as well. Mal seemed to enjoy it even though not a single guy there asked her to dance. Sammy kept her company, though. There were a few times I even got up and walked toward her with the intent to spend time with her, maybe even twirl her around a little. I never did.

Mal nudged me. "Hey, you okay?"

"Huh?" I blinked hard. The memories of her always consume me.

"You zoned out on me." She nudged me with her shoulder again.

"Sorry, just thinking of something." I stood and held my hand out to her. "As much as I would love to stay out on this deck and ravage you, I can't. Too many eyes. So let's go inside. Frankie will apologize and you will forgive him like you always do."

"You sure you can't ravage me?" Mal looked up at me through her eyelashes.

Fuck, I was rock hard.

I scooped her up into my arms and jumped into the water with her in my arms. She screamed, but didn't try to get out of my gasp. I swam under the dock with her to get out of the view of everyone. The sun was already setting, and they couldn't see us from the lake house.

"Maybe I could ravage you a little." I winked.

I bent down and kissed her. Fuck, her lips were so sweet.

Mal wrapped her arms around my neck and pressed her body to mine. The kiss became more urgent. I needed more of her.

I gripped her ass and pulled her to me. I could feel her heat through my shorts.

A voice from above yelled, "Rex! Mal! Where are you guys?"

It was Jake. Fuck. Not that he minded me having some of her as well, but there were limits. Anything below the belt, we all had to be there. It was only fair.

Mal went to swim into view when I grabbed her and shook my head. I just wanted a few more minutes alone with her.

"Mal! Rex!" Jake shouted again before walking away.

"Why didn't you tell him we were down here?" Mal whispered. "I mean, he knows about the hookups."

"Maybe I wanted to be greedy for a minute." I grabbed her and kissed her again.

Our lips danced against each other. The rush she gave me was better than any tackle I had ever had. And that includes a tackle that won us the state championship. She owned me in that kiss.

As our hands roamed one another's bodies, I needed more. I wanted all of her. She wrapped her legs around me and she ground up and down on me in the water.

"If you don't stop, I will take you right here." I dug my fingers into her hips to stop her.

"So, do it." She licked her lips.

"I have to wait for the others."

"Was this all planned?" She dropped her legs.

"Was what?" I looked around as if she meant something besides hiding under a deck and having a make-out session.

"You three. I mean, you guys don't even seem to mind that there is one of me and three of you. Honestly, I'm getting the better deal here." She averted her eyes. "Not that I'm saying there is a thing here. It's just well we have hooked up and now you say it has to be all three for ya know."

"Nothing was planned. But we all want you." I opened my mouth to say more, then shut it again. "Let's go back to the house."

"We were in the middle of a conversation." Mal crossed her arms.

"And that conversation will be finished later." I swam out from under the deck.

She followed after me and climbed up the ladder on the side of the deck. The water clung to her shorts and shirt, making them even tighter, showing off every curve of her body. Damn, she was gorgeous.

CHAPTER 17

Mal

I DIPPED MY HEAD UNDER THE BATH WATER IN AN attempt to drown out my thoughts. I didn't want to talk to anyone, nor was I in the mood to hear anyone talking. Rex was a comfort, but only a brief distraction as I tried to work out my father and brother's betrayal.

When I walked into the house, Frankie tried to talk to me. Instead of hearing him out, I went to my room and locked the door. Yeah, I was being childish, and I didn't care. Sammy, Jake, Matty, and even Rachel tried talking to me. I shouted through the door that I needed a minute. Really, I needed a lifetime to collect my thoughts.

How could my father move on? How could my brother not tell me? Today of all days, my father decided to spend it with some woman instead of with his children. How could he? Anger boiled in my veins. I pushed my face out of the water, gasping for air.

There was a faint knock on the door. Why couldn't they leave me alone? I sunk back under the water.

Arms reached around me, pulling me out of the water. Jake pushed my hair from my eyes.

I gasped.

"What are you doing?" He pulled me into him.

"Taking a bath." I wanted to be pissed at him, but his arms were so comforting. "You know, the door was locked."

"I'm sorry. It's not locked now. I just want to talk to you," he sighed.

"I said I needed a minute. I appreciate the concern, but please give me time." Pushing away from him, I sank back under the water. I knew I was being childish, and I was desperately trying not to be.

"Mal, please." He pulled me back to him.

"Jake!" I pushed away from him again.

"Talk to Frankie, please. Is this really how you want to end today?"

My face burned, and I bit my lip to stifle the tears that threatened to fall. I was aware of Jake's gaze and I desperately wanted him to think I was mature beyond my years. Someone who would be the bigger person in any situation. So, instead of giving in to the desire to cry or scream, I just sat up straighter and tried not to show any emotion.

"You're right. I'll go talk to him." I pointed to the sink. "Can you grab my towel?"

"Actually, I prefer you like this." Jake winked at me.

As I pushed out of the tub, he gave up and handed me the towel. I wrapped it around myself and walked into the bedroom.

"After I talk to Frankie, I would like to speak with you, Matty, and Rex." I slid on a pair of underwear without removing the towel. Yeah, Jake had seen everything, but I was still a little nervous about being naked around him.

He pressed his chest against my back. He was still wet from pulling me out of the tub. His breath was warm against my neck.

"You want to finish what we started?" He nibbled my neck.

Fuck. I was soaked, and I had just put on the underwear. It was my last clean pair.

"I said talk, not that." I spun in his arms to face him.

"Well, both options are on the menu for tonight." He kissed my forehead.

"Good to know." I playfully slapped his chest.

"I gotta get outta here before I throw you on the bed and take you." He released me and turned to walk out of the room. "After you talk to Frankie, we will be there for you."

When I walked into the kitchen, Frankie was already seated at the table, his hands crossed in front of him. Two beer bottles had been drained and left on either side of an uneaten plate of food, a testament to the amount of time he had been waiting.

"Were you waiting for me?" I sat across from him.

"Yeah, and also getting up the courage to go talk to you if you didn't come out of your room." He drained another beer bottle and added it to the other two.

"Why didn't you tell me?" No use in beating around the bush.

"I knew you would be upset." He shrugged.

"Of course I would be. How could Dad move on? And you didn't say anything."

"He cried every night for a year after mom died. Then he became a robot and distanced himself from everyone. You know how unbearable he has been to live with. Losing mom crushed him." Frankie got up and grabbed another beer from the fridge.

"It was hard on all of us. That doesn't mean you move on." I ground my teeth.

I hid in my room for weeks after she passed away. Reading books was my only form of escape. At times, I almost forgot my entire world had fallen apart. That still didn't mean I would ever replace my mother. Yet, somehow, my father had.

"He didn't move on." Frankie raked his hand across his face. "He just found someone that helps him."

"Dad replaced mom." I pushed my fingernails into the meaty part of my palm.

"You don't get it. It's possible for him to still love Mom and fall for another person." He picked at the mac and cheese on his plate.

I slumped into the chair. I knew all about loving more than one person. How could he know I did? There was no way he could know. My chest was heavy and cold, like something wet was pressing down on it. Of course, he knew. I was fooling around with his best friends. The top of my head pulsed in pain as if someone had jabbed me above my ears with a dull hatchet.

At some point over this weekend, he had to have seen us. Why else would he bring up being in love with more than one person? The way he said it was as if he knew. Wait. He said it more as if he personally knew the pain. Not that he knew what I was up to.

"This isn't about Dad," I accused.

"What are you trying to say?" Frankie cut his eyes at me.

"I think you know," I whispered. I wouldn't break Sammy's trust, but that didn't mean I couldn't try to get him to tell me.

"Actually, I don't." He slammed his bottle on the table. "Are you just trying to argue with me? Geez, this is why I didn't want you to come."

"So nice you would have left your little sister at home, alone, on the anniversary of mom's death because I'm a bother!" my voice was shaking as I was yelling.

"Stop being so dramatic." Frankie shook his head. "Sometimes I just want to do my own thing."

Frankie stood and paced the room. He kept opening his mouth to talk and then he would shut it again. At first, I didn't reply because I was so angry at his statement, as if I was always dramatic. But after he started pacing, I remained silent because I could tell he was trying to tell me something.

"Look, I just wanted time with Rachel. I know you don't understand what I mean." He blew out a long breath and sat back down. "Can we start over?"

Frankie may have thought I didn't understand, but I did. He didn't want Sammy there, and inviting me meant she would come. He was faithful and would never do anything with Sammy while he was with Rachel, but I was guessing that didn't stop his feelings. Ugh, I really wanted to hate him. I couldn't.

"Yeah, of course." I grabbed his hand.

"Listen, I'm sorry I didn't tell you about Dad." He squeezed my hand and released it.

"You should have, but I forgive you." I grabbed his beer and drained the rest of it. "So how long? Who is she?"

"A few months. He met her at some work conference. That's all I know." He got up and took two more beers from the fridge.

Lately, I had been putting my liver through the ringer. After this weekend, I would have to give it a break and stick to water. If it wasn't for the talk I was about to have after this one, I would have refused it. Instead, I chugged half of it down before it hit the table.

"Woah, slow down." Frankie chuckled and did the same to his.

"Hey, I almost broke my ankle today. I deserve all the beer," I huffed.

"Good point. You have had a pretty bad day. Maybe you should go to sleep before anything else crappy happens." Frankie shook his head.

CHAPTER 18

Mal

It was well after midnight when the knock came. I had texted Jake to wait until Frankie went to bed so he wouldn't catch us all in my room. Even if we had come up with a good excuse, I doubted my brother would believe us. Really, there was no reason for all of us to be in there.

Sammy had checked in to make sure I was doing okay, but I quickly shut her down. I told her I needed some time alone and asked her to stay in another room. There was a spare no one was using, and I was pretty sure Frankie had her and me together, so neither of us could hook up with any of the guys. She winked at me and left.

Poor Sammy, I knew she was suffering with seeing Frankie and Rachel together, yet there was nothing I could do to help. If there was a chance for them to be together, it would happen without me interfering. As for the moment, Frankie was with Rachel and that relationship needed to take its course.

I shook my head in an attempt to focus. There was so much I had to say to Jake, Matty, and Rex. The problem was, that I had no clue how to say it. Everything had gotten so screwy. Maybe if they all weren't leaving, things would be different, but they were.

Not to mention the fact that there was something between all four of us. Something more than just a physical attraction. Ugh, how was I gonna talk to them? I should have drunk more.

"Hey, hot stuff." Jake stepped into the room, followed by Rex and Matty.

I let out a breath I knew I was holding. This was going to be hard or awkward, probably both. Chewing my lip, I paced and waved for them to sit on the bed.

All three of them sat on the bed and stared at me. Their gazes warmed every inch of my body. I wanted to take them all. Shit, why did they have to be so sexy?

"What's up, babe?" Rex asked. "You look a tad terrified. Are you okay?"

Great, I didn't look all confident and cool like I thought I did. So this was gonna be even more awkward. Ugh.

Just spit it out. "I can't have sex with you guys."

A silence grew around us. I waited for them to say anything. They just stared at me as if I hadn't spoken.

"Did you guys hear me?" I knew I had said it, but were all three of them not paying attention?

"Of course." Matty sat up straight. "I was just trying to think of a response. I mean, you have every right to say you don't want us."

"I'd be lying if I didn't say I was disappointed that you don't want to, but it's okay." Jake smiled at me.

"Exactly what they said." Rex winked at me. "Hey, at least it's all of us. I would be crushed if you did one of us and left the other two out."

I burst out laughing. "I love the all-or-nothing attitude of you guys."

"We have all wanted you for years. So yes, it's all of us. Unless you pick just one of us. Really, it's your choice." Jake leaned back on his elbows. Shit, I wanted to climb on him.

"Oh trust me, I want all three of you guys," I spit out.

"So, what's the problem?" Matty asked.

"You guys are all leaving at the end of summer." I turned away from them, unable to look them in the face. "I'm already attached to you guys. If I, ya know, I... well...it'll be even harder to say goodbye."

"So, it's just the sex?" Rex asked. "Like the rest is cool?"

I bit my lip as I turned around to face them again. Fooling around with them without having sex seemed like a great compromise. As much as I wanted to, I wasn't prepared to give them my virginity. Not when they were leaving in two months.

"Truth or dare?" Jake licked his lips.

Enough truth was said for one day. "Dare."

"Be a good girl and kneel in front of Matty." Jake cocked his head toward his best friend. My cheeks grew hot as I looked at Matty. He was already grinning at me, his eyes dark with desire. I wanted to obey Jake's command, but a part of me was scared. What if it got too intense? What if I couldn't handle it?

But then I looked at Jake and Rex, their eyes both filled with lust. I couldn't back down now. Slowly, I got down on my knees in front of Matty. He leaned back on his elbows, giving me full access. I could feel the heat radiating off of his body and the scent of his cologne filled my nose.

"Yes, that's it. Now suck his cock." Jake's words came out smooth like velvet.

I leaned forward and pressed my lips to his stomach, feeling his muscles tense under my touch. Slowly, I worked my way down, leaving passionate kisses on his skin. Matty groaned and tangled his fingers in my hair as I reached for his waistband.

With shaky hands, I undid his belt and pulled down his

jeans, freeing his hardening length. His cock stood at full attention, straining against the fabric of his boxers.

I hesitated for a moment before taking the plunge, wrapping my hand around his thickness and pulling his boxers down. His cock sprang free, and I paused to admire it for a moment before taking it in my mouth.

Matty let out a deep groan as I suckled on him, my tongue swirling around his tip. I could feel him getting harder in my mouth, and I knew it wouldn't be long before he came.

I could hear Jake and Rex whispering to each other behind me, their words indistinct. It didn't matter. All that mattered was Matty's cock in my mouth and the knowledge that I was giving him pleasure.

As I continued to work on him, I heard the sounds of the others approaching me. Hands wrapped around my waist, unbuttoning my shorts. I continued to suck on Matty as my shorts were pulled down to my knees, followed by my underwear.

Scruff rubbed against my thighs as lips caressed my pussy lips. Since Jake and Rex both had a few days of growth with their beards, I wasn't sure which one it was. I gasped as their tongue ran along my slit.

"Oh, my." I kept my focus on the cock in my mouth. I had to, otherwise, I wouldn't be able to resist the urge to stop and focus only on the pleasure assaulting my pussy.

I swirled my tongue around, then pressed my lips onto his tip, swirling my tongue around his slit. Matty groaned and tangled his fingers in my hair. I could tell he was close to coming.

"Shit, I gotta come." Matty gripped my hair tighter. "I can't hold on any longer."

"Do it." I sucked harder. That was all it took for him to shoot his load into my mouth.

He fell back on the bed, panting. "Damn, that was intense."

Before I could pay any more attention to Matty, the intensity of my pussy returned. I looked between my legs to see the top of Jake's head. So it was him licking me.

Rex's hands reached around me and went up my shirt to my nipples. He played with them as Jake continued to devour my pussy.

Shit, I was already so close.

"Truth or Dare?" Rex groaned.

"Dare," I panted.

"Be a good girl and cum for Jake," Rex whispered in my ear.

"But not too loud. We wouldn't want anyone to hear." Matty sat up and kissed me.

I moaned into his mouth as my hips rocked against Jake's face. Fuck, I was about to explode.

Rex rubbed my nipples as Jake sucked my clit. My orgasm hit me hard and fast. My hips jerked as wave after wave of pleasure coursed through my body.

Matty deepened the kiss so my moans were muffled. Once the last waves of the orgasm receded I leaned back. Damn.

"Holy shit," I breathed.

CHAPTER 19

Mal

As I packed to head home, my mind kept replaying the night before. Actually, it was the entire weekend with them. I had fantasized about it so many times, I still couldn't believe it happened.

"Hey there, man-killer." Sammy flopped on the bed. "How did it go?"

"Huh?" I grabbed a pile of clothes and shoved them in my bag.

"Oh no. Don't you dare!" Sammy yelled at me.

"Dare what?" I stared into my bag.

"What?" She practically coughed on her spit. "Sleep with three gorgeous men and act like you didn't."

My head snapped up. I grabbed a shirt and tossed it at her. "Hush, someone could hear you."

"Okay, but I still want details," Sammy whispered, tossing the shirt back at me.

"There are none." *None that I'm willing to give you.*

"I saw all three of them come in here last night. Are you really gonna deny it?" Sammy sat up and glared into my eyes.

"They came in here, but I didn't sleep with them." I

averted my eyes again. She didn't need to know the details of what we did.

"That's a relief. So what were they doing in here?" Frankie asked.

I jumped.

He had come in and neither Sammy nor I noticed. Oh my, how much did he hear? Fuck, he was gonna hate me and his best friends.

"Probably checking on her after you kept secrets from her!" Sammy yelled at him. Whatever had happened between them still stung her.

"I didn't ask you." Frankie crossed his arms.

"Hey babe, don't be so harsh to her." Rachel came up behind Frankie and wrapped her arms around him.

"I don't need you to defend me." Sammy got up and stormed out of the room. "But thanks," she called out behind her.

"I told you she is a bitch." Frankie pulled Rachel in front of him.

"Don't talk about her like that!" I snapped at Frankie. "As for your friends. Yes, they were checking on me. After what you did to me."

"Then why are you glowing if that's all they did?" Frankie waved his hand at me. "You are yelling at me and yet I see the smile on your face."

Frankie was right. I was glowing. I stuck to my story and finally, he left and didn't bring it up again. As far as the smile, it remained on my face for the next month.

We snuck around every chance we got. If I wasn't at work, I was with my men. Ha, my men. I loved the sound of it.

Sometimes I would get all three of them. Other times I would get two or even one. They never seemed to be jealous of each other and they never tried to get me to ditch the other two.

It didn't matter to them what we did. One night, we went down to the lake and watched the stars without saying a single word.

Another night we had a Twilight movie marathon. I know, cheesy, but it was my guilty pleasure. Of course, my other guilty pleasure was them. Try watching the big fight scene with a man between your legs, distracting you the entire time. It was great.

Matty would cook on the nights that I wasn't working late at the restaurant. He was an amazing cook, making those some of my favorite meals. One night he made spaghetti from scratch because he knew how much I loved pasta. It was amazing.

Jake would spend his time with me, making me laugh and having long conversations into the night. He had an opinion on everything. Especially the way his father's business should be run. I wasn't sure about the logistics, but it seemed like it was rather profitable and a great opportunity for Jake. The major thing that I loved about our conversations was how well he listened. I could talk for hours about how one day I wanted to style famous people's hair and he would tell me how possible it was.

I even went to a few football scrimmages with them. Rex had to be careful not to injure himself, so they played two-hand touch football instead. I wasn't too sure about the rules, it all looked like a lot of running around to me. Frankie had questioned why I was there. I had a feeling he was more upset that Sammy had come with me.

That entire relationship had grown even more awkward. Or maybe it was because I knew something had gone on between them. Sammy wouldn't come over if he were there with his girlfriend. Since Frankie was always with Rachel, Sammy didn't come over much.

I should have been a better friend to Sammy. Instead, I

used the time to sneak around with Jake, Matty, and Rex. Frankie was too caught up with Rachel to even notice. At least that's what I assumed. Part of me wondered if he didn't notice because he was avoiding Sammy.

Because of his avoidance, he had become a clingy boyfriend to Rachel. He even brought her along on his work adventures. Every party he threw, she was there. Not that I went, but my guys kept me informed. They were worried about Frankie. I was too.

It wasn't just Frankie I was worried about. I was worried about Sammy and Rachel. Poor Rachel was in a love triangle and she didn't even know it. Sammy was so heartbroken she hadn't hooked up with anyone. I missed her stories of debauchery.

When I would talk to Jake about Frankie, he would tell me to stop worrying. Which, of course, was impossible. How could I not worry? The times I brought up Sammy to him, he didn't understand. Which made sense, for most people it was normal to not have random hookups almost every weekend. The problem was, Sammy wasn't like that.

Even with my concern for them, I was having the time of my life. There was no way I could be this lucky. Three wonderful guys giving me pleasure beyond anything I could imagine and yet they were all okay with not having sex.

A few times I had come close to saying screw it and well, screwing. I didn't. Thinking about having sex with them brought back the one bad thing about this entire arrangement, that one day it would end. I couldn't handle it.

I knew that at the end of summer, I would have to give them up. Until then, it was my summer with them. There was no way I was going to dampen it by thinking of its ending. At least, that was how it was going for the first month.

Rex broke the news to us that he would be gone for the weekend to go tour the University of Florida. He was already accepted, but the coach wanted to make sure he felt comfortable when the semester started. I had no choice but to face the reality. They were never mine. I had borrowed these men until they went about their lives once the end of August hit. I hated it.

CHAPTER 20

Mal

I DASHED AROUND THE DINER, FINISHING UP MY tables. It was my short shift and Matty was picking me up for a late-night dinner and cuddling. Rex was in Florida, and Jake was helping Frankie with a party. So date night was only Matty and me. I loved the rotating and the fact that they always made sure I had at least one of them around. Unless it was a girls' night, then it was just Sammy and me.

One table that normally ran late was walking out the front door. Yes, I would be outta work sooner than I had originally thought.

After swinging by the hostess station to remind Paula I was done taking tables, I went to turn in my singles. Paula just glared at me and didn't acknowledge me. For the past few weeks, she had been acting strange toward me. Sammy told me it was in my head.

"So, what are your plans for tonight?" Sammy asked as she wiped down the ketchup bottles.

"Me, Matty, and what I'm sure will be a fantastic meal," I smirked at her.

"I still can't believe you are dating all three of them." She grabbed a drink tray. "I love it."

"Well, not dating. It ends next month," I sighed.

"Why is it ending? Have you thought about long distance?" Sammy cocked her head at me.

From the corner of my eye, Paula walked by with a few menus and a couple following her. She did the unthinkable and sat them in my section. Why would she do that? I had never done anything to Paula, and it was like she was intentionally sabotaging me.

I stomped right over to Paula, who was standing at the hostess's desk with a huge smile on her face.

"I asked you not to sit me anymore. My shift is over." I crossed my arms.

"Oh, I didn't know. Maybe you should have been more clear." Paula popped her gum at me as if none of this phased her.

"I came over here and told you," I sighed. "I have a date tonight."

"Oh, with which guy?" Paula rolled her eyes at me.

"Huh? Why should that matter?" I asked.

"Gee, I don't know. Maybe because I had been trying to get Rex's attention all summer. But no, he only has eyes for you. I wouldn't be so hurt, but you are playing him. When he isn't around, you are with Jake or Matty. Do these guys know you are playing all three of them?" Paula's voice was growing louder with each word. "Let me not even get into how they all fawn over you in front of each other."

I stared at her, unable to speak. She was jealous. Yeah, Rex was a great catch. All three of them were. Was I supposed to choose between the three of them? How could I? Plus, they didn't mind sharing. Not that any of that was Paula's business.

"Nothing to say?" Paula snapped her fingers in my face. "Not surprised. Spoiled brat. I hope they realize you are playing them. Maybe then Rex will realize I'm the girl for him."

"I am not even gonna try to argue with you." I shook my head and walked away.

I didn't normally have issues with other girls. For the most part, I got along with everyone. Yeah, Sammy was the only friend that I was close with, but everyone else was always cordial with me. Maybe that was because they had never had a reason to be jealous before.

Squeezing my eyes tight and pushing aside thoughts of Paula, I went back to the servers' station. Sammy was still there cleaning the ketchup bottles.

"What was that all about?" She asked when I approached her.

"Paula is a bitch and sat me. Can you please take them?" I gave her the biggest puppy dog eyes that I could muster.

A loud crash and screaming came from the back of the restaurant. Sammy and I ran to the kitchen to see what was going on.

Richie, the cook, was standing there screaming at Barb, the manager. From what I could assess, it looked like he had tossed a large stack of plates on the floor. What I had thought was blood at first, was pasta sauce that was smeared over Richie's apron and the floor.

"I have told you numerous times that you can not be high at work!" Barb was screaming at Richie.

"I'm not!" Richie grabbed another plate and tossed it on the floor for effect.

"Aside from the powder under your nose, you left your stash on the prep station!" Barb pointed behind her to where Richie and the other cooks prepped the food.

"Whatever. I quit!" Richie turned around, grabbed a small baggie from the prep station, and walked out.

Sammy and I jumped into action, grabbing rags and the

broom. I was sweeping up shards of plates while Sammy wiped down the pasta sauce that littered the kitchen.

Barb stood there with a rag over her mouth, just staring at the mess that Richie had left behind. Although she looked shocked, she shouldn't have been. He was the third cook this year and more unreliable than the other two. He was never on time and took smoke breaks in the middle of the dinner rush.

"What am I gonna do?" Barb fanned her face.

"Are you two gonna work today?" Paula stepped into the kitchen. "I have been serving drinks to your customers and they all wanna order."

"Mal, go take care of the customers. Sammy, can you start the ticket orders that you know? As soon as I finish up, I'll jump in and do what I can." Barb took a deep breath and grabbed the broom from me.

So much for date night with Matty. I walked back into the main dining room without another word. Anything I wanted to say would have been nasty words toward Paula. She couldn't have predicted Richie walking out, yet I still blamed her for it.

Paula whistled as she went back over to her hostess desk. Yeah, she was way too happy about this.

I pushed aside all negativity and went over to my tables. While taking orders and clearing plates, Matty walked in. I gave him a quick nod but went back to work. Sammy had a few tables that I had to cover and although most of mine were gone, a late-night rush was heading in.

Four more tables headed in before I even had a chance to put in the tickets from my table and Sammy's. There was no way I was ever getting out of here.

Matty was still standing off to the side when I finally had a chance to talk to him. I hated having to tell him that our night was ruined.

"You okay, babe?" he asked when I approached him.

"No. Richie, the cook, quit. Sammy is cooking and now I have all these tables. I'm really sorry, but I have to cancel tonight," I sighed.

"Anything I can do to help?" He pushed some of my fallen hair behind my ear.

"No, but thanks." I kissed his cheek. "I appreciate it. Sorry about tonight."

"Don't worry. You go do what you have to do." Matty grabbed my hand and kissed it.

From the corner of my eyes, I saw two more tables come in. What the heck? I sighed and went back to work. Paula was no help. Instead, she sat people as quickly as they walked in and didn't bother to get their drinks. Staggering the seating would have helped me catch up. *At this rate, not only would I drown in the weeds of tables, I would never catch up.*

Running from section to section, I tried to serve all the customers. It took a few minutes to get all their drinks, and a customer yelled at me because they were ready to order and I wasn't ready to take their order. I wanted to be accommodating, but I also didn't want people to wait for their drinks.

Once I got everyone a drink I started taking orders. I grabbed the first two tables and rushed to put them into the kitchen. Of course, they wanted soup, which was something I had to grab. Normally, I didn't mind, but I was so far behind.

Stepping up to the pass-through for the kitchen, I put the two orders in and turned to rush back out to the dining room.

"Who haven't you gotten orders and drinks for?" Sammy asked as she fast-walked beside me.

"Aren't you cooking?" I asked as I went over to the soup station.

"Matty and Barb are." She jabbed her thumb behind her.

"Huh?" I spun on my heel, almost knocking the ladle out of the clam chowder.

"Matty went into the kitchen, told Barb he could cook, and told me to go help you." Sammy shrugged.

"Yeah, he can cook, but not like professionally." I dished out the two clam chowders.

"Right, because our last three cooks were professionals? This is a diner, not a steak house," Sammy laughed.

"Good point." I placed the two soups on a tray. "Okay. I only have booth's 7 and 13's orders. Wanna split down the middle and get these people served?"

"Absolutely!"

I rushed off to booth seven to drop off their soup before tackling the rest of the room. Had it not been so busy, I would have been able to process that Matty just landed himself a job with me. This was one wild summer.

CHAPTER 21

Mal

I wiggled on Rex's lap as I watched the movie. To be honest, I wasn't even sure what was playing. Having Rex's arms around me was such a distraction, I could barely think.

Jake and Matty were sitting on the sofa next to us, enjoying The Exorcist. Everyone agreed that since Rex had been gone all weekend, I got a little extra one-on-one time with him. Not that it would ever be enough. Ugh, I didn't know how I was going to survive without them. We only had a few more weeks left before they started leaving.

"What's wrong?" Rex whispered in my ear.

"Nothing," I whispered back, keeping my eyes on the screen.

Rex turned me to him. "Something is wrong."

Matty paused it and turned toward me. Jake and Matty were studying my face, probably trying to figure out why Rex thought something was wrong.

"Can we just watch this?" I didn't want this type of attention on me.

"After you tell us what's wrong." Jake crossed his arms and gave his best attempt at being stern.

"I don't want to talk about it." I tried to slip off of Rex's lap, but he kept his arms tight around me.

"Well, you should have thought about that before going and getting three boyfriends that care about you," Matty smirked.

"My boyfriends for a few more weeks," I sighed.

"Oh, babe." Rex cupped my face with his hand. "Please don't think about that."

"I've been trying not to. Do you guys have any idea how hard it is not to?" I looked down at the carpet, paying too much attention to the sauce stain.

Jake's mom turned the basement into an entertainment room for him when he was a teenager. She wanted him to have a place to hang out. Since she was out of town this week, it was the perfect place for us to spend time together.

"Yes, we all know how hard it is. I just think about how wonderful it is to have you for now." Matty tossed the popcorn into the air and caught it in his mouth. "Not to mention I get to work with you now."

It had only been two days with him, but it was perfect. He was a quick study and Barb was already saying that she never wanted to let him go. Matty was a fast, amazing cook. But that wasn't why I enjoyed working with him. Every time I walked by him, he would blow me a kiss or wink at me. The way he constantly flirted with me at work made me want to pick up extra shifts.

"That's unfair. We should get extra time with her because she gets to see you more." Jake grabbed the bowl of popcorn from Matty.

"It's not like I get to fuck her at work or else I might agree to that." Matty winked at me as if he had thought of taking me at work.

"We gotta live in the moment." Rex kissed my forehead. "I know it's hard. Trust me, we all have way too strong of feelings for you. Always have."

My heart slammed into my chest with his words. What exactly did he mean by strong feelings? Did he feel the same way I did? Before I had the chance to mull over what he said, his lips were on mine.

I deepened the kiss as I grabbed the back of his head. He was right. I had to live in the moment. And at the moment, I had three men who wanted me. A moan escaped my lips as I kissed him.

He picked me up and turned me so that I was straddling him. As he rolled my hips against him, another set of hands wrapped around me and pulled my shirt off. I pulled back just enough to see that it was Jake. He did have a thing for my tits.

Each one of my men had a taste for certain attributes of mine. Jake loved my breasts and exposed them every chance he had. Rex was more into my ass as loved grabbing it and grinding against me. Matty, on the other hand, had a thing for my legs. He would run his tongue from my ankle to the inside of my thigh. Then the way he would lick me, oh my, I was soaked thinking about it.

Jake threw my shirt on the floor next to the sofa. He brought his mouth to my nipple and gently flicked his tongue across it, sending shivers down my spine. I moaned again. My nipple hardened in his mouth and he sucked it harder. Then he switched to my other one. I reached back and grabbed the back of his head. He nibbled on my tits, causing me to gasp.

I kissed Rex again, and he gripped my sides, grinding me into him further. I giggled as I kissed him. When I pulled back, he smiled. "You're gorgeous."

He kissed me again and bit my bottom lip. He pulled me so close that I could feel his erection against me. I rubbed myself against it. He moaned as Jake sucked my other nipple.

Matty lifted me off of Rex and pulled off my shorts. I shifted so they would easily come off. He left my blue lacy thong on and set me back on Rex. As I grinded into Rex's erection, Matty was kissing my legs.

Jake continued to play with my nipples. I was so close to coming and none of them had even touched my pussy yet. Shit, my body was on fire.

Rex reached between his legs and unzipped his pants, releasing his thick cock. Matty eased me up enough for Rex to rub his cock against my pussy. My panties were already soaked. The roughness of the material, along with him rubbing himself against my clit, sent tingles throughout my body.

I looked down in just enough time to see Matty hook his finger into my panties and move them to the side.

"Please," I begged.

"Are you sure?" Matty asked. "We can just tease. You don't have to."

"I want to. I want all three of you."

Rex angled his cock at my opening, and Jake pushed me onto him.

Fuck. He slid in, filling all of me. I gasped as he pushed deep inside me.

"That's it. Be a good girl and take all of him," Jake growled as he pushed me down further.

Rex gripped my hips, grinding me onto him even further. I was so close to exploding. Matty pushed me back and he and Jake sucked on my nipples as my pussy adjusted to Rex's cock. That's all it took. I moaned as tingles raced along my skin. I exploded.

"Good girl, cum on my cock." Rex lifted me slightly and pushed me back onto him.

I tried to rock myself on him and I couldn't. He was in control. Lifting me and pushing me back down. My body was on fire. Every inch of my skin was covered in lust and perspiration. Fuck, it was so good.

Rex continued bobbing me up and down as Jake, and Matty kissed every inch of my body. I wanted to please them as well, yet my mind couldn't catch up. I was floating as Rex kept pushing his cock inside me.

"Ready for my cum?" Rex asked as he ground himself into me.

"Yeah," I whispered, barely able to talk.

As his dick twitched, he pulled me off of him just in time for his stream to hit me in the chest between my breast. His warm stream kept coming, coating my chest. I ran my finger along the cum and brought it to my lips, tasting his salty sweetness.

"Fuck, Babe. That's so hot." Matty grabbed me and lay me on my back on the floor.

I wasn't able to catch my breath before he was inside me, filling me. I moaned as he slowly rocked in and out of me. His fat cock spread my walls each time he plunged into me. I clawed at the rugs, trying to grasp at anything to hold steady. Yet, again, I was floating. Fuck, he was teasing me with his slow entry and then plunging deep inside me.

Rex came up beside me with a towel, wiping up his cum from my chest. I wanted to tell him to leave it, but each time I went to talk Matty would plunge deep inside me, silencing me. Fuck.

Jake pushed my legs up so Matty would get further into me. Each time I thought Matty was going to speed up, he would go slower, tormenting me. The grin that spread across his face let me know he was doing it on purpose. Every atom of my body was responding to the torture.

"Think you can handle both of us?" Jake pulled out his cock and started stroking it. "I can't keep watching. I need to feel you."

"I...c...can try," I gasped.

Matty placed his hands under me and rocked me upward so I was straddling him now. I started to grind against him, but he was already setting me back down. This time instead of my back being against the carpet, it was against Jake's muscular chest.

Rex squirted a fair amount of lube into Jake's hand. Jake reached between us and, from what I could feel, he rubbed some of the lube around my tight asshole. Oh, that was what he meant by both. They were gonna split me open.

Slowly, Jake rubbed the tip of his dick around my asshole. As he teased me, my body perked up. I wanted him. I wanted to feel what it was like to have two of them inside me at the same time. He continued to tease me, each time pushing his dick slightly into my asshole. I was opening up for him. I moaned, begging for him to enter me.

As Jake worked on entering me. Matty remained still, keeping my pussy filled with his cock. My heart raced as each moment I became more and more filled with Jake. Fuck, they were definitely gonna split me open.

"Such a good girl." Rex pushed my hair off my forehead and leaned in for a kiss.

While he was kissing me, Jake was fully entering me. I moaned into Rex's lips as the other two slowly fucked me. Had I known this was what Jake meant, I might have said no. As tingles erupted through my body, I was glad I didn't know. My heart raced as every atom of my being blended with them. It was amazing.

This was the first time any of them had touched my asshole, and I was glad they waited until I was ready. Jake grinded into my ass as Matty continued to tease my pussy. More tingles erupted.

I clenched, about to explode. Fuck, I was ready to cum. My

breathing increased as my heart pounded into my chest. I tried to grab at anything and managed to clutch Matty's shirt. He grinned as he continued to slowly move in and out of me. Jake followed Matty's rhythm, so they both pushed into me at the same time.

"Such a good girl taking both of us." Jake grabbed my breast as he plunged into me again.

"Are you gonna cum for us?" Matty licked his lips.

"Fuck," I moaned.

Rex clenched his fist in my hair, forcing me to look into his eyes. "I wanna watch you cum."

That's all it took. I fell over the edge. Moaning as the trembles crawled over my skin. I couldn't catch my breath, everything felt so amazing. It was as if I floated outside my body and came crashing back down into it.

Before I could control myself, Matty was pulling out of me. He unloaded himself onto my stomach. Stream after stream, he came onto me. At the same time, Jake's cock twitched inside my ass. He was coming inside me. I wished it was inside my pussy, but it was still amazing having him release himself into me.

"You are amazing, Love." Jake pulled out of my ass and gently set me beside him.

"I can't believe how amazing that was." I grabbed at my chest, still feeling my heart race.

"Time for a shower and then we can finish this movie." Rex scooped me up and carried me into the bathroom.

Yes, I was completely capable of washing myself, but I let Rex do it. He was so gentle and careful as he washed my aching pussy. His hands glided over my body with the soap, making it hard to not want him again.

Matty and Jake took turns jumping in the shower and washing themselves off. There wasn't enough room for all of us, but we made it work. The cutest thing was when each of them got out they kissed me on the cheek. They were the best boyfriends.

Pushing all thoughts aside of them leaving at the end of summer, I let Rex finish washing me and then I got out. He dried me off and even dressed me in Jake's t-shirt and a pair of his boxer shorts.

With a little skip in my step, Rex and I returned to the basement. They had pulled out the sofa bed and loaded it with pillows and blankets. Best sleepover ever. I snuggled in between them as Matty hit play again.

As I was drifting off to sleep, a loud crash came from behind me. Glass or something similar shattered against the wall. Tiny shards filled the air. A lampshade was clutched in the hand of someone behind us. Oh no.

"What the fuck is this?" The man who had just thrown the lamp asked.

CHAPTER 22

Jake

I JUMPED OFF THE SOFA AT THE SOUND OF THE LAMP breaking. That wasn't what had my heart slamming into my chest. It was the man who had thrown it.

Frankie. He stood there with a vein pounding in his temple. His jaw twitched as he stared at his sister. Yeah, she was covered up, but that wasn't the problem. She was here, cuddled up with his three best friends. Although Frankie was angry, I could see the betrayal in his eyes. Years ago, we promised to stay away from his sister.

"What are you doing here?" Mal whispered. She sat up and stared at him with big, bulging eyes.

"Me?" He pointed to himself with an envelope he was holding. "You have the nerve to ask why I'm at my best friend's house! Why the fuck are you in bed with all of them?"

"We were about to go to sleep." Matty shrugged, obviously not taking Frankie's anger seriously at all.

"I'm not in the mood for you, Matty!" Frankie shouted at him. "I'm not surprised at Mal. She has been pining after you guys for years. Kinda pathetic, if you ask me."

"Don't talk about her like that!" I stepped around the sofa and approached Frankie.

"Oh, that's cute. You are gonna defend her? You know it's true. She has been gaga over all three of you since we were kids! So, what? You three decided to take advantage of her?" Frankie took a step back from me as he was yelling, but he continued with his rant. "Let me guess, you guys take turns fucking her until you leave? Nice way to use my sister!"

"We're in love with her, you dumbass! Have been since we were kids! We were pining after her!" Rex approached Frankie from the other side, fists clenched, practically foaming at the mouth.

That was supposed to be a special moment, and it was said in rage. Of course, Mal had to already know how we all felt. It was pretty obvious we were all in love with her. Why else would we so easily share her? There was also the fact of how hot it was to watch her be pleased by one of my best friends.

I had wanted to tell her I loved her for a while. Truth was, I didn't know how to bring it up with all three of us leaving. It wasn't fair. None of this was. Mal was a lifetime girl, not a summer fling.

"Great. Have her fall even harder for you three. When you guys leave, I'll be here picking up the pieces." Frankie tossed whatever he was holding at Mal. "Fuck all you guys."

"Come on, Frankie. You're being unreasonable." I raised my hands to him in a non-threatening way. As much as I wanted to hit him for what he was saying, he was my best friend and Mal's brother.

"Mal, get in the car, I'm taking you home." Frankie nodded toward the stairs.

She grabbed her shoes and her purse. I tried to stop her, but the tears were streaming down her face. I called out to her, but she kept running. This was the one thing she didn't want.

Frankie was all she had left since she lost her mother and her father was never around.

Rex went to run up the stairs after her, but Frankie stepped in his way. "If we were ever friends, you wouldn't go after her."

"You need to calm down. You can't stop her from dating us," Matty said.

"Ha." Frankie leaned his head back and laughed. "You think what you three are doing is dating her? She's a place-holder for you guys until you leave. Just somewhere to put your dicks!"

My fist crunched into his face before I realized I had even swung. The blood poured from his nose as he stumbled back. I reached out to grab him and decided against it.

Matty and Rex each grabbed Frankie and steadied him. His hand reached up to his nose as he shook his head at me. Part of me was shocked I had hit Frankie and part of me wanted to do it again.

"You need to leave," Rex said to Frankie as he was pulling him up the stairs.

I wiped the blood that was on my knuckles on the side of my gym shorts and stood there staring at the wall. Yeah, it felt great to hit him, but how was Mal gonna handle that? Her one request was that he never find out.

What was he doing here, anyway? The envelope in his hand. I went over to where he had tossed it at Mal and picked it up off the floor. In the upper corner, it read Riva's Beauty Salon and School. Shit, it was her response to her application.

Instead of doing what I should have and chasing after her with it. I clung to it. At least it would ensure I would see her soon. Yeah, she would be upset about Frankie finding out, but it couldn't last long.

· · ·

Five days later, I still hadn't heard from her. Nothing. I had called and texted her numerous times without a response. Going by her house would be my next move if she didn't answer soon.

Even Matty hadn't spoken to her. Well, not really. She only spoke to him about work-related stuff. Anytime he brought up talking to her about what happened, she would shake her head and walk away.

"Guys, we have to fix this." I slammed my fist on the table.

Matty and Rex came by and brought a six-pack with them. I didn't need any more beer. The past few days I had drank myself to sleep. Yeah, I knew it was bad, but I had to do something to stop the pain in my chest from the absence of Mal.

"Agreed." Rex took a long pull of his beer.

"How? I can't get her to talk to me and I work with her now." Matty leaned back in his chair.

"I don't know." I shook my head. That was all I had been thinking about. We all knew how much she didn't want her brother to find out about us. Of course, he did. It was bound to happen. Mal may not have realized it, but we planned on keeping her forever.

"We need to get Frankie to approve." Matty tossed his hands up like that was the reasonable answer.

"Yeah, okay. That's not gonna happen." I crossed my arms.

"It has to. How else are we gonna get her back? He is the only thing in our way," Rex said.

"There is also the looming ending of the summer." Matty pointed his beer bottle at me.

Knock. Knock.

All three of us turned our heads toward the door. No one else was supposed to be here. My mother was out of town again on another business trip. I pulled out my phone and checked to make sure no one had texted that they were coming over.

I got up and answered the door. My mouth dropped as Frankie stood there. He had two black eyes and his nose was swollen. I grinned as I waved for him to come in.

He kept his hands in his pockets as he joined the rest of the guys in the kitchen. "Look, you guys are my family. I don't want to lose you guys, but you gotta stay away from Mal."

"Why?" Matty crossed his arms and glared at Frankie.

"Well." Frankie rubbed his hand across the back of his neck. "For starters, there are three of you. Come on. I may have understood one of my best friends with my sister, but all of them?"

"Sorry, but we all want her." Rex shrugged.

"No shit. I've known that you guys all had a thing for her for a long time." Frankie rolled his eyes and sat down.

"Then you know we can't just walk away from her." I sat down as well. As angry as I was at Frankie for Mal not talking to us for five days, I couldn't hate him. He was my best friend and looking out for his sister. The problem was that he needed to realize we were looking out for her as well.

"Come on. This isn't fair to her. Matty, you leave in what, two weeks? Rex the week after and Jake, what about you? When are you going to work at your dad's company?" Frankie sighed and looked down.

"Is that your issue?" I grinned.

"Well, part of it. I mean, I would rather none of you touched my sister, but if it had to be anyone, at least you all are good guys." Frankie raked his hand across his face. "And honestly, I'm tired of seeing her cry."

Yup, my heart ripped into a million pieces when he said Mal was crying. Anyone worth your tears should never make you cry, and yet she was crying. No matter what I had to do, I would make sure she never shed another tear again.

"I'm glad you are okay with this. Because we can't live without her." I leaned forward.

"But what about you three leaving?" Frankie asked.

"I have a plan." I clapped my hands together.

"Me too." Matty leaned forward. "I think. I'm kinda nervous about it, but I think it'll work."

"What plan? This isn't fair, guys. I have to go to Florida University," Rex pouted. "Oh, that's not permanent. I think I know what you guys are up to."

"Are you gonna fill me in?" Frankie scoffed.

"Okay, I'll tell you, but you can't tell Mal. Not yet." I leaned forward and filled him in.

CHAPTER 23
Mal

THE DOOR SLAMMED SHUT. I CRAWLED FURTHER under my blankets. Whoever was here it didn't matter. I had no intention of seeing anyone. It was my day off and I had one plan. Hide in bed all day.

Someone yanked at my comforter. I buried my face in my pillow. Why was anyone bothering me?

"Get up!" Sammy snapped.

Of course, it was her.

"I'm not playing!" Sammy yelled.

"Go away," I mumbled. "It's too early."

"It's four in the afternoon." Sammy flopped beside me. "You can't stay here forever."

I rolled over to face her. "I can try."

"No, you can't. I get it, your heart is broken. That doesn't mean you get to stop living."

"What are your plans?" I asked. We had spent so much of the summer talking about me that I had neglected her.

"Well, you know most of it. I'll be doing most of my business classes online. I only have two in-person classes, art and marketing. Then the rest of my time will either be at work or designing my all-sizes lingerie line." Sammy stared at the wall. She had dreamed of making sexier bras ever since she saw her mom's 42G bra and couldn't believe how utterly boring it was.

"How is all that going?" My stomach turned. I really should have shown more interest this summer.

"Same as always, girl. Could you get out of your head?" She shoved my arm. "You are acting like this is new and we never talk about me. We do, so stop it. Now get up and get dressed."

I sat up and looked at Sammy. She was wearing a low-cut black dress with silver strappy shoes. What the? "Um, why are you dressed up?"

"Your brother has a surprise. So get up. Actually, before you get dressed, go take a shower." Sammy clicked her heels together.

"I don't like surprises," I mumbled.

"I don't care. Get up." Sammy shoved me.

Letting out the longest sigh of my life, I slinked out of bed. Not a single part of me wanted to get up and do anything. If it wasn't for Sammy, I wouldn't have moved. She was all dressed up and giving me the big puppy dog eyes. So, of course, I was going to go. Whatever Frankie had planned didn't matter. I was still upset with him.

Knowing I wasn't allowed to date his best friends and getting caught by him were two totally different things. He knew I would choose him over them. It wasn't fair. He used my love for him against me and I was pissed at him for it.

Since I knew Frankie loved punctuality and would probably be expecting me to rush, I took my time. Twice while I was in the shower, Sammy knocked on the door to check on me. It took me roughly seventy-five minutes to shower. Well, I took a bath first and then showered. It was just to be spiteful.

When I finally emerged, Sammy was waiting for me with a

blow dryer and curling iron. One day I would be like her and be able to make someone feel beautiful simply by doing their hair and makeup. Of course, Sammy had a natural talent and I would have to study and learn. I didn't mind. It was worth it.

It only took Sammy thirty minutes to do my updo and makeup. Somehow she managed to curl every piece of my hair and have it cascade down my back. She even put little pink flowers in it. Tears streamed down my face and she immediately whipped them. It was the exact style I wanted for prom. Of course, I never went to prom. I pretended to have no interest in going, but after homecoming, I didn't want to risk rejection.

"No tears. You will ruin your makeup." Sammy reapplied the mascara.

"It's just so beautiful. Thank you." I grabbed her hands and stared into her eyes.

"Okay, stop it." She pointed to a chair. "Put on your dress and meet me downstairs."

"That's mine?" I gasped.

"Yeah. Hurry up." Sammy turned and left.

I slid on the dress. My hands rubbed up and down the sides. It was silky smooth, emerald green, and fit perfectly. Wow! I couldn't even believe I got to wear such an exquisite gown. Then I saw the box with a bow on it. It held a pair of black strappy shoes with red bottoms. Wow! I had never owned something so expensive.

Frankie had money, but I couldn't figure out why he would spend so much on me. Maybe he was trying to apologize for being such a jerk.

I put the shoes on and took baby steps. They fit perfectly but were the highest pair of heels I had ever owned. My stomach turned. Please don't fall. Please don't fall. I managed to get downstairs without tumbling down them. It was promising.

In the living room, Sammy sat on the sofa with Rachel and Frankie. Rachel was wearing a red number that almost outdid Jessica Rabbit. It was stunning. Frankie had on a black tux with a red bowtie.

"Okay, seriously, what is this all about?" I asked. Everyone was way overdressed, including me.

"It's a surprise." Frankie got up and held out his arm for me. "Let's go."

Rachel and Sammy got up and walked out of the house before I even took two steps. They were used to walking in high skinny heels. I wasn't.

"Before we leave..." Frankie turned to me and stared at the ground. "I just want you to know I'm sorry for everything."

"Please, not now." I fought back the tears. "I'm trying really hard not to hate you and if you... Just don't."

"Okay, let's go." Frankie led me outside.

I had no expectations. So when I saw the white stretch limo outside, I almost vomited. It was beautiful. Never in my life had I been inside a limo. Frankie outdid himself.

After quickly glancing at Jake's house and seeing no one was home, I slowly walked to the limo. Yeah, the shoes were not going to last. The driver was waiting by the door and he opened it for me and then held my hand while I scooted inside.

My mouth dropped. It wasn't the lights that ran along the edge, or the bottles of champagne on ice. It wasn't even the slow music playing. No, it was none of those super fancy things. It was the three men on the opposite side of the limo.

"Ahh!" I screamed as I tried to leap toward them. It was too confined of a space and I fell forward. Luckily, I wasn't too high up and I didn't hurt anything.

"You are so clumsy," Frankie snapped from behind me.

I paid zero attention to him. He was lucky I even heard what he said. My eyes were focused on my men. All three of my men were there. They all had black tuxes with emerald green ties.

Jake scooted over and helped me off the floor. Rex and Matty were quickly behind him and sat next to me.

"How?" I whispered.

"Frankie helped." Matty grabbed my hand and kissed my knuckles.

"Why?" My head spun.

"Because he knows how we feel about you." Rex kissed my cheek.

Jake opened a plastic box with small pink rose buds inside it. It was a corsage. "Will you go to prom with us?" He slid the corsage onto my wrist.

"I'm so confused." I took slow, steady breaths.

"We didn't get to take you to prom, so Frankie helped us set up a prom for you. Well, for us." Jake kissed both of my hands.

Tears swelled in my eyes. None of it was real. There was no way it could be. Frankie was very clear about me not dating his friends. I looked around the limo. He was sitting there smiling and holding Rachel's hand. Sammy sat closer to us and kept her gaze away from Frankie.

"If you mess up your makeup before we even get there, I will kill you." Sammy leaned forward and handed me a tissue.

"It's just. It's well." I dabbed at my eyes.

"Accept that this is real." Frankie handed me a glass of champagne. "I'm not too happy about it, but obviously you four are happy and how can I deny my sister and best friend's happiness?"

I took the glass and drank it in one gulp. "Thank you."

After what was only a short ride, the limo stopped. The driver got out and opened the door for us. I scooted out of the limo with the help of Jake and Sammy. We arrived at the warehouse that Frankie sometimes used for his parties. I crossed my fingers that my vomit was no longer visible on the side-walk. Luckily it had been months and all traces of it were gone.

Inside I was once again surprised. Round tables with blue and gold linens lined the dance floor. A DJ stood in the corner with all of his equipment. It was all decked out and gave prom vibes. There was even a sign above the stage that said The Make-up Prom.

"Get it. Like we are making up for the lost prom." Matty pointed to the sign.

"It's beautiful." I dabbed at my eyes again. "Seriously this is all too much."

"You deserve the world." Rex winked at me.

Flashes went off in my face. I blinked until I realized a woman with a camera was directly in front of us. Jake pulled us over to a wooden archway where she continued to take photos of us.

Before I knew it I was being whisked onto the dance floor. My three men took turns twirling me around and pulling me in close for certain dances. It didn't take long before I had to sit down and remove my shoes.

It was the most magical night of my life. Sammy must have invited Trevor Montgomery from lit class because she was on the dance floor with him. Frankie and Rachel slow danced to every song no matter the beat.

After about an hour Harry, Donnie, Billy, Larissa, and Gabby showed up dressed in proper prom attire and took off to the dance floor. None of them gave a second glance at me with three men. I guess part of me thought it would be awkward. They didn't seem to care.

"Thank you," I said to Jake as he swirled me around. I planned on thanking each one individually.

"I love you," he blurted out. "I can't go to New York City. I've already talked to my dad and he is gonna allow me to work remotely. Some weekends I will have to fly out there, but I'll work that out. That is if you want me to stay here."

"Really?" I stopped moving and stared directly into his eyes.

"Really. So, Mallory, will you have me?" He pulled in close.

"Of course." I wrapped my arms around his neck and kissed him. "I love you too."

"Can I cut in?" Rex tapped Jake's shoulder.

Jake winked at Rex and stepped out of the way.

Rex grabbed my waist and swung me around. "So, I'm guessing you said yes to Jake."

I nodded.

"Good. If I could get out of my commitment to Florida, I would. It would destroy my career if I did." He glanced at the floor.

"I know. I would never ask you to do that," I whispered.

"Well, if you'll have me. I would love for you to come down on some weekends and I can come up on holidays. I know long distance sucks, but at least you wouldn't be alone." Rex chewed his lip. "I already talked to the coach and he said they would pay for your flights and a room while you are there."

"Why would they do that?" I gasped.

"Because I'm that good." He grinned.

"Well of course I'll come visit. I love you." I licked my lips. It was true, I was in love with all three of them.

Rex scooped me up and spun me around. "I love you, too."

Matty stepped in as soon as Rex set me down. "Wanna play a game?"

"You and your games," I giggled.

"Yes, but you are our favorite game." He grinned.

"So what's the game?" I asked.

"You move in with me. I'm taking over Rex's apartment while he is gone. Jake plans on moving in as well." Matty smiled. His words came out in a joking manner, but nothing of what he said was a joke.

"How is that a game?" I couldn't wrap my head around what he was saying. "And what about Harvard?"

"We could play house. Get it?" Matty took a deep breath. "Okay seriously. I'm madly in love with you and I can't imagine going to Harvard and you staying here. Don't give me that look. Barb offered me the full-time cook position. Cooking is my passion. Teaching will always be there. I can find a teaching job closer."

"I love you too. Which is why I can't let you do that." I choked on my words.

"It's done. So have me or don't, I'm staying." He pulled me in and kissed my ear. "I do hope you'll have me."

"You know I will." As much as I wanted to force him to go become a professor I couldn't. I wanted him. I wanted all three of them and they were all giving me a chance to have them.

All three of them stayed with me on the dance floor. We laughed and danced and enjoyed the moment. Sammy came over a few times to shake her butt on me. Then at one point, everyone there ended up in a circle dancing.

One by one someone would step in the circle and bust a move. We all cheered and laughed. Even with my lack of skills I entered the circle. As I was shaking it I looked around. There were two people by the entrance walking into the party. At first, I couldn't tell who they were, then I froze.

My father and Jake's mom entered the room, hand in hand. What the? My head spun.

"Wh...ho...uh..." I stuttered.

"Mal, relax. Dad knows about you and your boyfriends." Frankie stepped in front of me blocking my view.

"How?" I finally managed to get out.

"Jake's mom figured it out a while ago." Frankie shrugged.

"But why would she tell him?" My brain shook. My dad always being gone. Him being at her house the other night. Them holding hands right now. The woman he had been seeing. My father was dating Jake's mom.

Before I could speak, my dad entered the circle and held out his hand to me. "Can I have this dance?"

I wanted to say no. I wanted to scream and yell at him. Instead, I took his hand and danced with my father. He swayed us out of the circle and out of earshot.

"I know I haven't been the greatest father. Parenting never came naturally to me like it did your mom." He looked away from me but I still saw the tears in his eyes. "I know about you and them three boys. I'm not surprised. You always did crush on all three of them. It makes sense you guys all ended up together."

My mouth dropped. Had I been holding a million dollars I would have dropped each and every dollar all over the floor. He just gave his approval. No snide comments or anything.

"Now, I accept your life choices I need you to accept mine," he said.

There it was. His quid pro quo. No way he would have just done something without expecting something in return.

"I love Candace and I need you to be okay with that." He stopped moving and glared into my eyes.

No, you forgot all about Mom and moved on. I hate you. I hate everything about you. "Okay. It will take me some time, but I understand."

"Thank you." He pulled me in for a hug.

"By the way. Your brother told me about cosmetology school."

"Yeah, he said he got the envelope from Jake, but I haven't looked at it yet." I averted my eyes.

"Well, we did. Don't glare at me. We had to know how

153

much it cost. Obviously, you got in. And we paid for the whole thing. Well as long as you don't fail any classes or any clinicals. Then you would have to pay for extras." He pulled away from me as if judging my expression.

"You didn't have to do that."

"It's done. You deserve it." He kissed the top of my head and walked away toward Jake's mom.

The rest of the night was spent eating, dancing, and all around having an amazing time. Every time I blinked I had to remind myself it was real. I had the loves of my life, my dream school not only accepted me but was paid for. And now that my dad came clean about Miss Matthews he would be around more. It was perfect.

Once the night wore down, everyone said goodbye and gave me hugs telling me how happy they were for me. Jake, Rex, and Matty escorted me to the door. Once outside, Rex scooped me into his arms since I wasn't able to put my shoes back on. He placed me in the limo and the rest followed.

"Where to now?" I didn't want the night to end.

"Home," they all said simultaneously. "Our home."

The End.

Note from the Author

I can't express how thankful I am for all of you. This journey is such a pleasure and I enjoy writing these stories of strong women finding their true loves. This one in particular was so much fun to write. I wanted a light-hearted romance and the love between Mal and her men provided just that. Please join my Facebook group and drop a pic of what you think her men look like.

Till Next Time, Muah
    Callie

Also by Callie Sky

The Triplets and The Blonde

Bought By Three Men